THE GIRL NEXT DOOR

CHELSEA M. CAMERON

carina
press

carina
press®

Recycling programs
for this product may
not exist in your area.

ISBN-13: 978-1-335-14694-6

The Girl Next Door

Carina Press
22 Adelaide St. West, 40th Floor
Toronto, Ontario M5H 4E3, Canada
www.CarinaPress.com

Printed in U.S.A.

To anyone who has been thrown a curveball in life
and caught that sucker, this one's for you.

THE GIRL NEXT DOOR

Chapter One

Iris

I smelled the ocean before I saw it. I took the long way back; the scenic route. Anything to prolong the inevitable. Turning my car onto a back road, I sighed as I rounded a corner and drank in the view of blue waves crashing over the rocky shore, coating the rocks and turning them dark. This was my home, whether I wanted to admit it or not. I'd started my life here in Salty Cove, and now I was back.

All too soon, I reached the turn for my parents' road. *My* road now. It took everything in me not to start crying when I pulled into the driveway and shut off the car. Time to face my new reality.

"We're here," I said to the snoring gray lump in a crate in the backseat. "Can you please wake up and comfort me right now?"

With that, my Weimaraner, Dolly Parton, raised her head and blinked her sweet blue eyes at me.

"Thank you."

I got out of the car and went into the back to let her out of the crate. She jumped out and shook herself before sniffing the air.

"I know, you can actually smell the ocean here. It's not covered up by city smell. At least one of us will be happy with this situation."

Dolly started snuffling the ground and then found a spot to pee while I looked up at the house. Why did it look smaller? I hadn't been here for months and in that time, it had shrunk. The white paint peeled in places, and the flower boxes on the wraparound porch needed watering. I hoped the garden out back wasn't in as bad a shape.

The side door opened and out came my mother carrying a chain saw. She didn't look at me immediately, but then she did and her face broke out into the most brilliant smile that made her look years younger.

"Hey, Mom," I said.

She put the chain saw down on the porch before opening her arms. "Welcome home, baby girl."

I forced myself not to cringe at the nickname. I was twenty-two, hardly a baby at this point.

Still, I let myself be folded into her arms, and I drank in the familiar scent of fresh-baked bread and fresh-cut wood.

She rubbed my back up and down and then leaned down to pet Dolly, who lost her shit and lapped up the attention.

"A tree came down last week, so I've been cutting it up. Come on in and see your father. You can bring your stuff in later. He's been antsy to see you all day."

I looked back at my car, which was packed to the roof with all the shit that I had left after I'd sold most of everything in a last-ditch attempt to cover my rent.

Mom put her arm around me and started filling me in on town gossip, but a loud rumbling distracted me. I turned my head in time to watch a sleek black motorcycle pull into the driveway next door.

"Is that—" I started to say, but then the rider got off the bike and pulled off their helmet, shaking out their short dark hair.

"Oh, yes, that's Jude. Her parents moved down to Florida and left her the house."

Jude Wicks. I hadn't seen her since she graduated four years ahead of me in school.

Jude didn't glance in my direction as she covered the bike, jogged up the steps, and slammed the front door of the house. I jumped at the sound.

Dolly whined and I looked down at her.

"Her parents left her the house?" I asked as Mom and I walked up the steps and into the house. We didn't have air-conditioning, so fans were doing all the work, just blowing around the semi-moist sea air.

Mom was distracted from answering by Dad yelling at her from his recliner. He'd hurt his back working for the power company for thirty-five years and was retired. They relied on Mom's income as a real estate agent and substitute teacher.

"Iris is here," Mom called to him.

"Baby girl!" he yelled when I came around the corner.

"Hi, Dad."

I went over to give him a huge hug. Dolly immediately put her chin in his lap and whined for attention.

"Hello, Dolly," Dad said with a chuckle, setting his coffee down next to a stack of library books beside his chair.

"What are you reading now?" I asked.

He held up the book he'd rested on the arm of the chair to keep his place. "Started reading these young adult books. This one's about these kids who are planning a heist to steal this magic stuff. You can have it when I'm done."

Mom poked her head in and asked me if I wanted some coffee. "Sure, thanks."

I sat down on the couch as Dolly curled up at his feet and closed her eyes.

Mom brought me a cup of black coffee and some creamer. I added enough so that the coffee turned from black to khaki. Perfect.

"How was your drive?" Mom asked.

We caught up on my trip, the fact that she'd cleared out my room for me, and what else was happening in town. Mostly it was about who my parents knew that had died, what they had died from, and talking shit about a few while simultaneously hoping they rested in peace.

Less than an hour at home and I already wanted to escape, but I was stuck here, at least for now.

I had to unpack my car, find a place for Dolly's food and water bowls, and settle into my room. Luckily for me, my brother, who was ten years older, had vacated it a long time ago to go to college.

My bed was small, but Mom had bought me a new mattress recently, so there was that. Still, it was a twin bed, when I'd been sleeping in a queen in my apartment. That had been left on the street. No one wanted someone else's mattress. The bed frame had been taken by Natalie, one of my former coworkers. I missed her already, and needed to text her that I'd made it home safe. She was so worried about me moving back to Maine that she'd literally bought me bear spray. I told her that the likelihood that I would die from a bear attack was slim to none, but she wouldn't listen.

The walls started to close on me as I looked at the tiny bed. Sure, I'd had to share my old apartment with someone I didn't like, but my bedroom had been twice this size, and I'd had two big, beautiful windows that looked out on a courtyard filled with flowers and butterflies and twittering birds. Maine had all those things, but it wasn't the same.

To add insult to injury, none of my sheets or blankets were going to fit the bed. I added that to the list of things I needed to get with money I didn't have.

Dolly followed me into the room and climbed up on the bed. She took up most of it.

"I'm going to end up on the floor," I said to her. She closed her eyes and huffed out a sigh.

I sat on the edge of the bed and looked around. At least the posters I'd had on the walls in high school were gone, and the room was freshly painted white. My window looked out toward the ocean, which sparkled at me beyond a row of trees. At least I could see the ocean every day here.

My phone buzzed with yet another text. Natalie. I sent her a quick message that I'd arrived safe and had not been mauled by a bear. I ignored the message from Anna, my old roommate, about some dishes I'd apparently left behind and if it was okay for her to have them. Whatever. She could knock herself out. She'd stolen a bunch of my other shit, so I wasn't sure why she was contacting me about this. I considered blocking her number so I'd never have to speak to her again.

I reached out and stroked Dolly's velvet head. She leaned into my touch. "What are we gonna do?" I asked. She didn't answer.

Later that night, after I unpacked my car and had dinner that consisted of meatloaf, mashed potatoes, and a fiddlehead salad, I sat on the couch as Mom watched a reality talent show and Dad read.

This was my life now.

"What are your plans for tomorrow?" Mom asked during a commercial break.

"I'm not sure."

I hadn't thought any further than today. Everything else was a blank. I was always the girl with the plan, but now, I was adrift. An unmoored boat, lost at sea with no hope of rescue.

"I was talking to Cindy Malone the other day and they're hiring for summer help at The Lobster Pot," Mom said. "You did that in high school. I know she'd hire you. At least it would give you something during the summer until you can find something more permanent if you need to."

I tried not to make a face and instead grabbed one of the books on Dad's "to be returned to the library" pile. Another young adult book; this time a Cinderella retelling. I read the blurb on the back and if I wasn't mistaken, it was a romance between two girls. I was surprised that my dad would want to read that. I wasn't going to comment, though. I cracked open the book and started to read. Mom still stood waiting for an answer.

"Oh, uh, sure. I'll call her tomorrow," I said.

I mean, what else was I going to do? Go down to the local bar and take up day drinking? Hang out at the gas station with the local teens? Sit on the beach with the tourists and get a horrible sunburn? I tried not to think about what I could be doing right now, if I was in Boston. Maybe dinner and drinks or pizza with my friends, a hot yoga class at my favorite studio, or even just taking a book to a coffee shop to read for a while and watch people pass on the street. If I wanted to have a professionally made cup here? I'd have to drive at least ten minutes and they definitely didn't have nondairy milk or know what a macchiato was.

Not that I could even afford a macchiato since I was fucking broke, and I needed money sooner rather than later. Working at The Lobster Pot was my best option.

"Sounds good, baby girl," Mom said with a smile. Her

shoulders relaxed and she sat back in her chair. I realized she'd been worried. She seemed to be relieved I'd agreed to her plan so easily.

My parents and I hadn't really talked about what happened and why I was back, mostly because it wasn't for just one reason. There were many reasons, all culminating with me packing my shit in my car, loading up my dog, abandoning my friends, and driving back here.

I asked Mom if there was any ice cream in the freezer and she said that there was. While I was getting a spoon, I glanced out the window, which happened to look right into our neighbor's living room.

Jude.

The lights were on and she stood in the living room wearing nothing but a sports bra and some athletic shorts. The spoon I'd just grabbed clattered on the floor. As I stood up from retrieving the spoon, I found her staring directly at me. Instead of looking away like a normal person, I stared back.

Her hair had been long in high school and her arms hadn't been so...sculpted back then. At least not that I remembered. My mouth went dry and I held on to the spoon for dear life.

"What are you looking at?" a voice said behind me and I shrieked and dropped the spoon again. I turned around and found my mom leaning over my shoulder to see what I'd been staring at.

"Oh, nothing, just staring off into space." I rushed with my spoon and the ice cream back into the living room. My parents kept the room dark and the only light was from my dad's lamp and the TV, so I could hide in a corner with my lobster-red face.

What had come over me? I'd just stood there leering like a fucking creeper. Part of me expected a knock at the door and for her to storm in and ask what I'd been staring at.

That didn't happen, but it didn't stop me from looking up from my book every few minutes to check and make sure.

Before bed, I took Dolly out to do her business and my eyes kept flicking over to the house. The lights were still on, but I wasn't going to stare this time. I hadn't asked for more information from my mom about Jude, but I did wonder what she was doing back here. She'd hated this town, from what I remembered, so it couldn't just be because of her parents' house.

High school in a small town in Maine was brutal for anyone who didn't conform, and Jude had been adamant about not conforming. I'd done my best to get through, and the drama club had been my safe haven. I'd never thought seriously about acting after high school, since that was way out of my league, but I still thought about it every now and then. There was a community theater group a few towns away. Could I put myself out there and get into it again?

Dolly was taking her sweet time, sniffing the bushes at the edge of the porch to find the right one to pee near. I jumped as I heard a door slam, the door to the neighbor's house.

I froze with my back to the house, pretending I wasn't completely aware of what was happening. Was she leaving again on that motorcycle? Where would she go tonight? The only bar in town closed in less than an hour, and there was nothing else open. Unless she might be going to a friend's house for a party?

Or perhaps she was going to the beach for a midnight swim. I shivered at the thought of Jude slipping beneath the waves like a mermaid.

My ears perked for the rumble of the motorcycle starting up, but I didn't hear it. Dolly finally found her perfect spot and did her thing. She seemed content to sniff around the yard, so I let her, wrapping my arms around myself and breathing the sharp sea air. I'd missed this smell, even if I hadn't missed much else. Maybe I'd go for a midnight swim. The only danger of doing that in the height of the summer was encountering drunken teenagers, out having a bonfire on the beach and smoking a lot of weed.

I closed my eyes and took a few deep breaths before turning around. I told myself not to look at the porch next door, but my eyes had other ideas.

She was there, sitting on the porch on an Adirondack chair and staring out toward the ocean, just like I'd been doing. An open beer rested on the porch railing.

I swiveled my head away so she wouldn't catch me looking again, and at that moment Dolly decided that she'd make a mad dash for Jude's yard.

"Dolly!" I yelled as she bounded up the porch and went right for Jude. Well, shit. "Dolly, come back!"

She completely ignored me. I was going to have to go get her.

Groaning inside, I dragged myself over to the house, preparing for anything. What I found was Jude petting Dolly's head and Dolly closing her eyes in bliss and then trying to climb in Jude's lap.

"Dolly," I said, but she acted as if I wasn't even there. "I'm sorry. I should have kept her on the leash." I couldn't look up at Jude, so I watched her hands stroke Dolly's head. The air around the porch seemed thicker somehow, or maybe it was just harder to breathe near Jude.

"It's okay," she said, and I felt like I'd never heard her voice before. I wasn't sure if I had. "I don't mind."

Dolly finally stopped trying to climb into the chair and settled for putting her paws and her head in Jude's lap.

"Sorry," I said again. I needed to take Dolly and get the hell out of here, but I couldn't move. My feet were glued to her porch.

"Haven't seen you in a while, Iris," she said. Her voice had a rough quality that made me think of bar smoke and darkness. There was a hard quality about her that made my stomach flip over a few times.

"Yeah, I moved back today." My gaze finally crept its way up to her face only to find her watching me with fathomless brown eyes. Her face was all sharp angles, along with her haircut. A fluttering in my stomach erupted, and I forgot what we were talking about until she blinked again.

"When did you get back?" My voice trembled, and I hoped she didn't hear it.

Her fingers danced back and forth on Dolly's head. "Last year," she said, but didn't elaborate. Chatty.

"I should probably go," I said, stating the obvious.

"Stay if you like," she said, picking up her beer and gesturing to the empty chair next to her.

"Okay?" I collapsed into the chair and tried to calm my galloping heart.

"Do you want a beer?" she asked after a few seconds of silence.

"No, thank you." What was I doing here? I should have grabbed Dolly and run back into the house. Was Jude doing this so she could confront me about staring at her earlier?

I had no idea how to have a conversation with her so I stopped trying to think of things to say and just sat there, my insides twisting around like pissed-off snakes. At least Dolly was enjoying herself.

Jude didn't seem eager to say anything either, so there we were. I kept expecting my mom to open the door and yell for me to come back. At least that would give me an escape route.

Out of the corner of my eye, I watched Jude. She petted Dolly with one hand and the other lifted the beer to her lips periodically. She wore a T-shirt and the same shorts as earlier.

I needed to stop thinking about that earlier non-outfit. I blushed hard and hoped she couldn't see in the dark.

If I strained my ears, I could just barely hear the crash of the waves. Somewhere nearby, a soft boom followed by another let me know someone was setting off fireworks.

"That's a cool motorcycle," I blurted out, and wished I could walk into the ocean and disappear.

"Thank you. It's not very useful in the winter, but it's good for getting around in the summer." She pressed her lips together as if she'd said too much.

"I've never been on a bike. I'm scared I'd fly off or something." This kept getting worse and worse.

"I'm sure you'd be fine, once you tried it. Do you always let fear dictate your life?"

I sat up, shocked. "*No*," I said, but it didn't sound convincing. "You don't even know me." I didn't know her either, but I was the one being called out.

"True. Just something to think about." She moved Dolly's head and stood up. "See you later," she said, and went into the house, leaving me and Dolly wondering what the hell had just happened.

Dolly came over to me and whined.

"Let's go home," I said and she seemed to understand me. I got up with shaking legs and made my way back to the house. The lights were still on next door when I glanced back one more time.

Chapter Two

Jude

I tried to remember her, but since there had been four years between us in high school, the memories were hazy. She'd had friends, from what I'd seen, and seemed to do okay in that fishbowl environment. Not always fighting against the current like me.

I didn't know what she was doing back here, and I was trying not to care, but this was one of the first interesting things to happen in Salty Cove in a while. I also hadn't missed the way she'd looked at me earlier. Might be my imagination, but I was pretty sure I'd seen interest there, which was interesting on its own. She'd definitely been interested in guys, last I knew. I'd known that I liked girls, and girls only, from a young age. I'd refused to hide who I was and had come out at an age where kids were the most vicious. Still, I'd gotten through it but bore the hidden scars.

Not that I was going to pursue anything with her, even if she was interested. No, I wasn't ready, even now. It had been more than two years but not much had changed. Living in Salty Cove and fishing for lobster was like living in a space where time barely passed, where it moved so slow that you didn't notice and suddenly you were old and still living the same life you'd had for dozens of years, even though you swore you wouldn't. This town locked you in, made you forget that there was anything or anyone outside it.

I should probably get out more, but look what getting out of Maine had gotten me. I was back to the place I never wanted to be and I didn't have any plans about leaving. Where would I go? I'd lost everything. I was lucky to have parents who were thrilled that they could stop paying a property manager and get free labor from their daughter. Now they could spend their time soaking up the sun and drinking cocktails every afternoon in Florida. If I could stand to be with them, I might have joined them.

No, I don't think I could handle living in Florida. I wasn't really handling living here, but it was easier to float through my life in a familiar environment, even if that environment was so homogenous that everyone was related to everyone else. Except for me.

My thoughts drifted from my life here back to Iris. She'd clearly gone off to college and now she was back. I knew her father had retired with some injuries, so maybe that was why. Or maybe it was something else and she'd needed a soft place to land. This town was a safety net for so many people. She seemed a little frenetic, or maybe that was her personality. Nervousness radiated from her in waves. It didn't bother me, though, which was surprising. I normally gravitated toward people who were like me, reserved and quiet, but if she was going to be next door for a while, maybe we could hang out. I definitely needed more friends, since I didn't have anyone close, just acquaintances.

I'd touched on a nerve when I'd told her not to live in fear, but I'd done that on purpose to see what would happen. Chalk it up to boredom.

She was cute too, I'd have to give her that much. Wide-set blue eyes that had untold stories behind them underneath light brown curls. Her curves were generous and lush. No, I wasn't going to think about her body. Completely inappropriate. I hadn't thought about anyone's body *that* way since...

Everything always came back to that. To *her.* I couldn't even think her name without a stab to my heart.

If Iris was cute was irrelevant because I wasn't going to love anyone ever again. I'd done it once and once was enough. I'd gambled and lost, big time. Iris probably wasn't going to come back anyway, because I'd been rude and had just left her on the porch with her dog. I'd been afraid that she was going to start asking me personal questions, or try to talk to me, and I was out of practice talking to other people. That was the best part of my job: the no talking to anyone. Sure, there was the stink of bait and the hard physical labor, but every day when I went out, I got to be alone. I preferred being alone these days. It hadn't always been like that, and I still had friends who tried to get in touch every now and then. Some were persistent and kept trying, even when I gave them nothing. I guess there was something to be said for that. Too bad I was such a shitty friend. Maybe I could practice with Iris.

I finished my beer inside and put the TV on so the house wasn't so silent. I didn't really watch it, but the noise and color distracted my brain for a little while. Due to my job, I'd adjusted to a different sleep schedule, so after I put the bottle in the recycling, I stripped off my clothes and headed to bed. I slept with the windows open and the sound of the ocean doing its best to lull me to sleep.

My eyes closed and I felt myself float toward sleep on a soft current. It only lasted for a minute as my brain conjured her face and then I was wide-awake and trying not to cry. They weren't nightmares, exactly, but they did keep me from ever getting a good night's sleep. Most of the time my job exhausted me so much that my body would sort of shut down anyway and I'd take a nap or two in the afternoon, but for the most part, I didn't sleep.

After trying about six different sleeping positions, I got up and grabbed a blanket to sit with on the couch. I was learning how to crochet, which kept my hands busy and my mind thinking about stitches and counting and making sure I didn't leave a hole. I was testing out different techniques on squares, and eventually I'd put them all together as a blanket. At least, that was the plan. I was only on the second square, and my squares didn't exactly look like the pictures, but at least I was doing something. I'd burned through so many hobbies in the last two years, including puzzles, wire jewelry, baking bread, and raising succulents, to keep myself sane. Barely.

I curled up on the couch for a few hours of rest before my alarm went off. It was still dark when I got up and got dressed. I kept my regular wardrobe separate from my work wardrobe. I had to. You could never get the stink of bait out of jeans, let me tell you. I actually kept my work clothes on the porch so they didn't funk up the house. I tossed my extra jacket, boots, and oil pants in a bag on the back of my bike, packed up some protein bars and a sandwich, coffee, and water for the day, sucked down a protein shake, and I was ready for work. My bag was already packed with the other essentials: sunblock, a hat, gloves, a portable charger for my phone, and a few tampons. Just in case.

I spared one glance for the house next door, but the lights were all off, since most normal people weren't awake at this hour. At first, it had been horrible, waking before the sun. Now I relished this quiet. I often spent entire days where I only had to communicate in a few words or grunts. That probably wasn't healthy, but it was working for me right now.

I headed down to the wharf to grab my dinghy and row out toward my boat. I wasn't alone, and shared a few nods and waves and grunts with my fellow cohorts. There weren't a whole lot of women on the water, but the guys had never really said much to me. I was sure they had talked behind my back, but no one said anything to my face. Not that I would have put up with any bullshit from them. I'd been telling men off my entire life and needed more practice.

My shoulders popped and cracked as I rowed out to my boat, named the *June Marie*. I'd bought it from a man who had named it for his wife and daughter, as many did, and I hadn't been able to come up with a better name, so I kept it. Maybe one of these days I'd change it to something like the *Salty Bitch*, but then that would mean I was staying here and the boat was mine and this was my life now. I didn't want this to be my life. I used to picture my life in so many different ways, and now it was a blank. I was stuck, but I couldn't find the way forward. I wanted to dream again. I just didn't know how. Back in the day, I'd planned on getting my MBA and then opening a coffee shop or a greenhouse or a bar. I didn't know what my business would be. I just knew that I wanted to work for myself, and that seemed like the way to do it. I'd been young and naïve then.

The *June Marie* roared to life and I steered it out of the harbor. The first few days like this on the water had been spent acclimating to the waves and the up-and-down motion of the boat, but somehow, my body had stopped fighting it and I wasn't puking over the side while trying not to hit a buoy or a seal.

I always played music on the boat, so I turned on my favorite playlist. Lizzo blasted from the small speakers I'd rigged up in the cabin. It was cold as fuck today, so I wrapped myself up and sucked down half of my thermos of coffee as the sun rose. The forecast was for temps in the eighties later, a rarity for Maine. Right now the air was downright frosty. That wasn't something I had bargained on when I started. I'd learned a lot since then. A bunch of the guys I'd hung out with in high school had worked for their dads, and I'd helped out once or twice, so I wasn't completely new to fishing. I'd still had to fumble my way through at first.

I reached my first buoy, which was painted white with a black stripe around the middle. I hadn't been very creative there, I had to admit. I set about the nasty job of throwing bait into bags to re-bait the trap, and then the business of hauling the trap up from the ocean floor. If I wasn't such a small operation (only fifty traps), I might have had help in the form of a sternman, but then I would have had to talk to someone, and that would have been the worst. I'd rather curse and struggle and take longer doing things on my own than hire someone else. Plus, I'd have to pay them and I was barely making it work as it was. At least I didn't have to pay a mortgage.

I lost myself in the rhythm of my work: bait, haul trap, pull out lobsters, measure, rubber band, re-bait, toss back in ocean.

By the time most people were getting up for work, I was almost halfway through my traps for the day. I had two rotations and alternated them every other day. My body had grown used to the physical work, but I would never get used to the smell of bait and diesel. No amount of showers seemed to remove the smell. Guess that was another bonus of having a sternman: someone else got to do the stinky jobs.

I had a decent haul and headed back to the lobster pound, where they'd buy the lobsters right from the boat, boil them in the restaurant upstairs, and serve them all in the same day. I also threw a few in a cooler on the back of the bike for myself, since it was cheaper than buying organic chicken at the grocery store.

I hosed myself off near the dock and decided to head home instead of hanging out to shoot the shit with the other lobstermen. Sometimes I lurked and they let me hang on the edges of their conversations, listening but not contributing. They didn't seem to mind, since we were all in the trenches together. I could have joined if I wanted to, but I'd never tried and the longer I didn't try, the harder it became.

I stopped quickly to fuel up the bike and grab a fresh-baked croissant and another huge black coffee at the only gas station in town. It was also a variety store, stocking everything from guns to gummies to wedding gowns. Seriously. I didn't know who was buying said gowns, but they had them anyway.

The lobsters went into the fridge out back before I stripped completely and ran for the shower. I honestly didn't care if the neighbors saw me dashing through the house after I abandoned my clothes in the doorway. I didn't used to, anyway. Maybe now I should care a little bit about a certain neighbor seeing me completely naked. No, I wasn't going to think about that. I wasn't going to think anything. I was just going to close my eyes and try and wash off the smell of dead fish guts and also not think about anything at all. Nothing. I wanted to think nothing.

I wanted to *be* nothing.

Chapter Three

Iris

I barely slept at all that night, and it wasn't because Dolly hogged the bed and I had to find space for my body around her. I couldn't stop thinking about the odd interaction with Jude and what it could all mean.

By the time I gave up on trying to sleep and got up for breakfast, I hadn't found any more clarity.

"Good morning," Mom said when I came out to the kitchen. "I've got waffles going if you want some. I've got a showing later and then a meeting, so it's going to be just you and your father this afternoon."

I grabbed a strip of bacon from where it was drying on a paper towel and crunched into it. "That's fine. I'm going to go over to The Lobster Pot and see about the job and maybe go get some groceries."

Since I'd moved out for college, my diet had changed and I wanted to be able to make smoothies and salads and so forth. My parents were old school and thought eating massive amounts of vegetables and salad was a strange fad for weirdos who did yoga.

"Sounds good, baby girl." Mom kissed my cheek and poured some batter into the waffle iron. I asked if she needed help, but was promptly herded out of the kitchen. Dolly stood at the door, whining to go out. This time, I took her on a leash.

The motorcycle was gone already, so I didn't have to worry about seeing Jude.

I sighed and waited for Dolly. It hadn't even been a week and I was ready to murder someone for a brown butter hazelnut crunch donut from Union Square Donuts, or a peanut butter cannoli from Mike's Pastry, or a slice of puttanesca pizza from Regina Pizzeria. I was really hungry, apparently.

All my life, I'd dreamed of getting out of this town, of leaving and building a life where I could go to the grocery store and not everyone knew who I was. Boston somehow seemed less scary than New York, and I'd had my pick for getting a degree in marketing with an English minor. I'd wanted to work for either a nonprofit or for an ethical company focused on sustainability or environmentalism. I'd ended up working at a few startups and burning out, fast. I shoved those melancholy thoughts of my many failures away. I could wallow another time.

Dad hoisted himself out of his chair for breakfast, and I joined my parents at the table. They chatted about this and that, not really involving me in the conversation. My parents had gotten used to their empty nest, no doubt, and would also have to adjust to having me back here.

This was what I hated. I hated that my mother was making me breakfast and putting it on my plate, as if I was a child. I hated that I couldn't just leave the house without telling them where I was going and when I'd be back. I hated sleeping on a twin bed. I hated that my life didn't look the way I'd always planned that it would. By now, I was supposed to be living in my own apartment with a bay window that looked onto a courtyard. I was supposed to go to a job every day that I loved and that made me feel like I was doing good for the world. Instead I was eating waffles my mom had made me. Way to fall into those depressing thoughts again, Iris.

"You're awfully quiet. You okay?" Dad asked, touching my arm. I pushed the rest of my soggy waffles around my plate. "Yeah, just thinking."

Mom and Dad shared a look that only two people who have been married for thirty-plus years could share.

"You know you can talk to us about anything, right? We're here for you," he said. Mom got up and put her arms around my neck. "We love you, baby girl, and we're happy to have you here. Even if it didn't turn out the way you planned. You can stay as long as you want, okay?" She smacked a kiss on my cheek and I wanted to run away.

"Thanks," I said, but my voice sounded hollow. I didn't want them taking care of me. I was supposed to take care of myself. I was a fucking adult and I'd had to run home to Mommy and Daddy at the first sign of trouble. The "trouble" came when I was almost evicted from my apartment for failing to pay rent when I'd had to quit a shitty job and couldn't seem to find another one. I'd burned through my credit cards and had to throw in the towel.

By now, the whole fucking town knew I was back because nothing stayed secret here for more than a day. When I'd eventually go to the grocery store, certain people would come up to me and ask all kinds of questions, pumping me for more details while pretending they were just being kind because they wanted to know the dirt. My mom would also get inundated when she went to work at school and at the real estate office, and I wondered what she would say to everyone.

Before I could do anything, Mom cleared my plate and went to start the dishes. Dad went back to his chair, groaning the whole way.

"I'm off to work," she said, kissing the top of my head like I was five. She kissed Dad and whispered something to him that I couldn't make out. I had the feeling it had to do with me.

"I'll bring pizza home later, so don't worry about dinner," she called as she walked out the door.

"Great," I said under my breath.

★ ★ ★

I hung around with Dad for a little while, finishing up the lesbian Cinderella book before getting dressed in shorts and a tank to go to The Lobster Pot. I left Dolly with Dad, since she was conked out at his feet. He could keep her alive for a few hours.

I cringed when I saw my gas gauge because it meant one more chance I might have to interact with someone. I suppose I could have stayed in the house and not left for a week or more, but I couldn't handle that. I needed out.

For half a second, I thought about driving right back to the city, but I couldn't leave Dolly. No, this was my only option right now. Being here, in Salty Cove.

The pumps were busy at the only gas station in town, go figure, and the lot was full of pickup trucks all parked next to each other. Country music blared from one of them, and a pack of teenagers huddled together sipping beer from cans "hidden" in paper bags. Subtle.

I rolled my eyes and waited for a pump. Although I hadn't lived here for years, I bet I could name nearly all of the people in this parking lot.

Finally, a pump opened up and I pulled my sedan up to it, cringing at the prices. They were so much higher here, but nearly everything else was cheaper, compared to Boston.

I got my gas without having to chat with anyone, but I knew I wouldn't be as lucky at the grocery store, so I decided to hit The Lobster Pot first.

It was nearly lunchtime on a Saturday in June, and the

parking lot was full, but I found one spot way in the back. The little restaurant doubled as a wharf, and it was also the port for a local seal and whale watch tour boat. People walked up the rickety steps to the restaurant as others headed down to a tour boat, chatting excitedly about seeing whales. Families sat on picnic tables and cracked into fresh lobsters before drenching the meat in bowls of clarified butter. Now I was hungry.

I headed up the stairs to the restaurant, which didn't have an empty table in sight, and had a line out the door. Since I'd worked here ages ago, I walked right in and leaned on the corner of the counter. The open kitchen bustled with people pulling fries and shrimp out of the fryolater, grilling burgers on the enormous industrial grill, and calling orders out over the mic near the pickup area. Complete organized chaos.

I snagged a server who'd been cleaning the tables.

"Is Cindy around?" I knew she would be. That woman practically lived here.

"Yeah, I'll go get her," the server said, her eyes wild with the stress of keeping up with the summer crowd. I wanted to tell her that she would get through it, and to just breathe because I'd been there. Looked like I was going to be back in that place again, but at least I had some experience dealing with a rush like this.

Cindy came out a few minutes later, wearing a polo with the restaurant logo and an apron stained with grease over it.

"Iris Turner, as I live and breathe. Get over here and give me a hug, girl," she said, holding her arms out. I hugged her and inhaled the scent of butter and fried fish. Soon, I would smell the same. No matter how much I'd showered after I came home from work, the oil penetrated my pores and I'd smelled like that all the time.

"What are you doing back here?" Great, she didn't know yet, which meant Mom hadn't told her. Thank you, Mom.

"Yeah, I'm back home for a little while. Trying to figure out what to do next. My mom said that you were needing some help, which is why I'm here." Might as well get right to the point.

Cindy put her arm around me and pulled me into the back where her office was. "Come on back and sit with me for a little while. I'm dead on my feet." She collapsed into a rickety office chair, and I pulled out a folding chair that was propped up against the wall. The office was a mess of papers and a computer that looked older than I was and made a strange chugging noise as it struggled to keep working.

"It's real nice to have you back, Iris, and I would love to hire you on for the summer. You're an answer to our prayers, actually. We've been having a hard time getting help for some reason, and I won't even have to train you since you already know the ropes. When can you start?"

"How about tomorrow?" I needed to get busy and stay busy. I also had past due bills that were racking up late fees, not to mention my student loans.

"Perfect. How about you come in at ten and we can retrain you on everything before lunch. What size polo are you?" She reached into a box next to her desk and pulled out a red polo shirt that was exactly the same as what she had on, except it was clean.

"That looks fine," I said, taking the shirt.

"Here, take a few more, so you don't have to keep washing that one." Cindy loaded me up with shirts and then wanted to shoot the shit for a little while, asking if I was happy to be back and saying my parents were probably pleased to have me. I kept a smile on my face and lied through my teeth until someone came back and said they couldn't find any more straws.

"Duty calls," Cindy said, getting up with a sigh. She gave me a hug and told me she'd see me the next day and I died a little inside. I considered getting something to eat before I left, but the line was too long and I'd be eating this food nearly every day for the rest of the summer anyway.

The task of getting a job completed I braved the grocery store the way I did when I was in the city: with earbuds in and a podcast turned all the way up, and without making eye contact with anyone.

Five minutes after getting my cart, when I was trying to find a decent avocado, there was a tap on my shoulder. I wanted to ignore it, but I pulled out my earbuds and turned around only to find my third grade teacher. I put another smile on my face and did the chatty small talk until my teeth ached. I finally found two acceptable avocados and moved on to lettuce, then fruit. I had two more encounters by the time I made it through the produce, and then two more when I was buying dog food for Dolly. By the time I made it to the dairy aisle, I was worn out and wanted to shut myself in my room and not talk to another person for at least three days.

I checked out, and the bored teenager bagging my groceries didn't talk to me, for which I was grateful.

Dolly was waiting by the door when I got back home and about knocked me over. She was nearly as tall as I was on her hind legs, and she was a good sixty pounds.

"Easy, girl, I've got groceries here." I balanced the bags and tried not to tip over as she jumped up to lick my face.

I stumbled to the kitchen and dropped everything. I had wanted to do this all in one trip, and I'd succeeded. After petting Dolly and telling her how much she was missed, I put away the groceries. Dad shambled out of the living room to see what I'd gotten.

"What's this?" he said, holding up a package of chia seeds. "Isn't this what you put on those pottery things and it looks like hair when it grows?"

I gritted my teeth. "Yes, but they're also really good for you. I put them in my smoothies."

He made a grunting noise and dropped the container on the counter like it had burned him. I got a few more questions about other ingredients I'd bought. He also wanted to know what was up with the small blender I'd put on the counter to make smoothies. I answered him as patiently as I could before he refilled his water bottle, grunted again, and headed back to his chair. Sounded like he was grumpy and maybe having a bad pain day with his back, so I wasn't going to hassle him.

I took Dolly out into the yard for some exercise, bringing her favorite ball and the thrower that went with it.

The motorcycle was back, so Jude was home from wherever she'd gone. I wanted to ask my mom, because she would definitely know, but I didn't want to seem like I was actually interested in the answer, even though I was.

I chucked Dolly's ball as far as I could get it and she raced after it like a goofball, ears flying. I laughed as she brought it back. She danced just out of reach, getting down in her play position before running off again.

"Come back, you doofus! I can't throw it if you don't give it back!" I chased her and finally got the ball from her mouth, setting it back in the thrower before hurling it again. I should probably also take her for a walk up the road a little bit later. Maybe after dinner.

I tossed the ball for a while, wondering what Jude was doing and wondering if she could see me. Not like I was going to pose, or act different if she could. Dolly didn't show any signs of getting tired, so I was going to do this until Mom got home.

"Hey," a voice said behind me.

I swiveled slowly to find Jude leaning on her porch, wearing a white tank top over a black bra, and those same shorts from the other night. Or maybe she had multiple pairs of the same ones.

"Hey," I said, and it sounded like a question.

"Do you want some lobster?"

I couldn't answer for a second because the words didn't make sense. "Do I want lobster?"

"Yeah. I have extras and I don't want them to go to waste."

That was curious, because you could definitely cook lobsters and then have the meat for a few days. Or you could freeze them. But I hadn't had lobster in forever and the thought of it drowning in butter was making my mouth water. Mom was bringing home pizza, but lobster sounded much better right now.

"Sure," I said. I called to Dolly and walked over to what I was now thinking of as Jude's house.

"They're boiling now, but I can make lobster rolls or you can just take them if you want."

Huh. One of those things meant staying and having dinner with her, and the other meant taking the lobsters and running.

The choice was mine.

"A lobster roll would be amazing," I said after a few seconds. I was going to eat with her, if only to satisfy my curiosity about her life and what she was doing here.

"Cool," she said. "Come on in. Dolly is welcome too, of course."

Dolly dropped her ball at Jude's feet and wagged her tail, looking up at Jude. My dog had a crush.

"Thanks," I said, following Jude into the house. I knew I'd been in here when I was a kid when our parents hung out, but it had been a long time. This house was bigger than my parents' and definitely decorated in the New England style with lots of wood, plaid, camo, and if I wasn't mistaken, that was a deer head on the living room wall.

Dolly raced through the house, sliding on the hardwood and nearly crashing into a table.

"I'm sorry. She has no manners," I said, trying to grab her, but she was too fast. Her gray fur was shiny and hard to get a grip on.

"It's fine, let her go."

Dolly went right for the couch, sniffing it before hopping up on it and lying down, taking up almost the whole thing.

I rolled my eyes. "So, she's just going to make herself at home, apparently."

I followed Jude back to the kitchen, where she stood over a large pot of steaming water. She tucked some hair behind her ear. Her hair hung just below her chin in a bob that was longer in front and cropped close to her neck in the back. Attractive. Very attractive.

"I can do corn too, if you want," she said. "I wasn't really planning on having company, but I like to cook a bunch of whatever I'm eating and then I have leftovers in the fridge. Do you want a drink?"

"Sure, why not?"

Jude cracked open a beer and handed it to me. I wasn't much of a drinker, but I drank in social situations. This seemed like the kind of night where a drink was a nice addition.

"Thanks," I said and took a sip. The beer was crisp and light. Not bad. "Do you need any help?"

Jude shook her head and checked on the pot before yanking out four bright red lobsters and putting them in a colander in the sink. I watched as she dumped out the rest of the water and filled it up again. Her arms flexed and muscles popped along her shoulders and back, and I had to look away. Where was Dolly?

"Why do you have so many lobsters?" I asked.

"I'm a lobsterman." She hefted the pot and put it back on the stove. I almost slid out of my chair.

"You're a lobsterman?"

"Technically lobsterwoman, but yes." She checked the burner and then turned around to face me.

"Wow," I said, because what else did you say to something like that? "So *that's* why you have so many lobsters."

"Occupational hazard," she said with a shrug. "It's mostly because I'm lazy and I happen to love the taste of lobster. I also bring home clams a lot too. You'd think after over a year of doing it, that I'd be sick of them, but not yet." She dropped several ears of corn in the pot and then went to clean out the lobsters.

"Are you sure I can't help?" I was feeling completely useless.

"I'm assuming you know how to crack a lobster," she said.

"Seeing as how I spent five summers at The Lobster Pot, I'm going with yes." I took a lobster cracker from her and stood at the sink next to her. "Race you?"

She arched one dark eyebrow. "You're on."

We each picked up a lobster and looked at each other.

"Ready, set, go!" I said and went for the claws first. I'd never speed-cracked a lobster, but this was my moment. I'd done this plenty of times before, so I was confident in my abilities. After getting the claws and knuckles clean, I went for the tail, sliding the meat out in one piece. I turned to declare my victory. Jude had already finished with the first lobster and was working on her second.

"Fine, I see how it is," I said, dropping the tail into the bowl.

Instead of going for the other lobster, I watched her crack her second. Her hands were just so efficient. I wondered briefly if she had calluses on her palms or fingers. From all the lobster trap hauling. What a mental image *that* was. Jude, all decked out in the waterproof orange overalls and boots and maybe a tank to show off her arms and shoulders. Before I could take a headfirst dive into that fantasy, I said I'd chop up the lobster meat for the lobster rolls.

Jude checked on the corn and pulled out some celery, chives, mayo, lemon juice, and buns. I was used to simple white hotdog buns, but Jude had some brioche from a local bakery.

"Wow, these are going to be classy," I said as she buttered the rolls and gave them a quick grill in a skillet, while I chopped the celery and mixed it with the lobster meat. "Am I in charge of mixing and measuring?" I pulled some of the corn out of the pot.

"Yeah, go for it. I'm guessing you've made a lobster roll before."

I had. I'd made hundreds. Maybe thousands. It was pretty simple and you didn't mess with a classic. I mixed everything up in the bowl, and then Jude brought the buns over. I assembled the rolls and she added corn to our plates.

They were definitely inherited from her parents, like the rest of the house. Off-white plates with dark blue trim, each chipped in multiple places, and a few had clearly been glued back together. Looking closely, I could see a faded print of what might have been a rooster in the center, but it was hard to tell.

"Thank you," I said, and we sat at the dining table. I heard my mother's car pulling into the driveway next door and sent her a quick text that I was over at Jude's having dinner and to save me some pizza. Then I turned my phone off. I'd deal with the questions later. Right now I was starving, both for food and for more information about Jude.

"Thank you so much for inviting me over," I said again, picking up my first lobster roll.

She licked some stray mayo from the side of her hand. "Thank you so much for accepting. It's been a long time since I had dinner with anyone else in this house."

I wanted to ask her if she was lonely, but I didn't want to pry. No, that was a lie. I did want to pry, but I didn't want her to think I was rude. Big difference.

"Why did you come back?" I asked. Oops. Didn't mean for those words to come out of my mouth so soon. I shoved the lobster roll in so I wouldn't blurt out anything else that would cause her to throw me out before I'd finished eating.

Jude picked up an ear of corn and started to eat it carefully. I was like a toddler when I ate corn. I got butter all over my face and usually a few kernels ended up in my bra and it was all a disaster. Jude ate as if she had been taught to eat by a proper British monarch. She hadn't answered and I started to feel like this had been a mistake.

"Sorry," I said as I chewed. "I didn't mean that to sound like an interrogation. I can tell you why I'm back. Because I'm a fucking failure." I took another huge bite and chased it with a swallow of beer. Perfection. Why hadn't I had this combination before?

Jude didn't comment on my outburst. Just kept eating her corn and keeping eye contact with me. It was eerie, the way her eyes seemed to give me an anchor while everything whirled and stormed in my brain.

"I did what you're supposed to do," I continued. "I went to college and got a fucking degree and then I couldn't get a decent job that would help me pay my rent and then I got more into debt and then I got to the point where it was get evicted or come home. I did everything right and went to school for marketing, which everyone said was a guarantee, but all of those people are fucking liars. And do you know how hard it is to get someone to rent you a decent apartment that isn't infested with roaches, or is bigger than a shoebox? No one tells you about that shit. And then when you can't pay your rent, there's no backup plan. It's too bad, so sad, sucks to be you. I would have died before I asked my parents to bail my sorry ass out, even if they had any extra money, which they don't. So I came home and now I have a job at The Lobster Pot and I have no idea what I'm doing with my life except cleaning up my dog's poop and this is nothing how I thought my life would be and that fucking sucks." I heaved a breath as if I'd been running up the stairs.

"Life never happens the way you plan it to, does it?" Jude put down her naked ear of corn that had been stripped of its delicious kernels by her clever teeth.

"What did you think your life was going to be?"

She laughed darkly, and I shivered at the sound. Jude's laugh was pure sin. I closed my eyes for a second to compose myself. "I thought I was going to kick the dust of this town off my feet and never come back. I didn't care where I went, as long as it was anywhere but here."

Our eyes locked and I had one of those moments when you connect with another person and they can feel it too, and you don't know anything else in this world but how that person understands what you'd been through. They got it. Jude got it.

"Same," I said. "I was only going to come back for Christmas and funerals."

"I wasn't even going to do that," she said, picking up her first lobster roll. She took a bite. "This is really good. Perfect amount of mayo and pepper."

"Thank you." The compliment made my cheeks get hot. "So, why are you back?" I asked. I wanted to know. I needed to.

"That's a question with a lot of answers and I'm not sure I'm ready to share them. I can hear them whispering about me at the bank or the library. I know how this town works. Everyone wants to hear about it, but I get satisfaction from keeping that little mystery to myself."

That made complete sense. Whispers and gossip stuck to you like superglue and you couldn't shake a reputation, once it was created in someone's eyes. They put you in a box, and you could set that box on fire, but they would leave you in it even if you burned alive.

Jude finished her first lobster roll and moved on to the second while I went for my corn.

"You could tell me," I said. "If you wanted to share it with someone. I'm not going to tell anyone. They're talking about me too."

I shuddered at the thought. It wasn't just that I'd come home in disgrace after moving away. Being queer in a town like this meant that you were constantly talked about as well, and not in a complimentary way. I hadn't come out until my senior year of high school, and even that had been a nightmare. I'd waited until just before graduation so I could say "bye bye fuckers" and never see any of those people again. Yet here I was, hiding from them in a restaurant a few years later. My parents had been pretty nonchalant about the whole thing, and most of the adults in my life really didn't seem all that pressed about it. At least not any of the ones I ended up coming out to, like Cindy. A few people, like the queen bee bitch in school, Marina, had been spreading rumors about me being queer for years and greeted my coming out with smugness. From what I'd gleaned from social media, she'd gone off to college in New York, but had come back to work for her parents who made stained-glass windows and Christmas ornaments. I'd had to avoid her at the grocery store last time. In a town this size, I didn't know how long a conversation with her could be avoided.

Jude had been out her whole high school career. I still remembered some of the words people hurled at her like rocks in the hallways. I'd only been a freshman, but I remembered. Sure, there were other people who were out and our school had a GSA, but that didn't stop the local homophobes, and their parents, and their grandparents. It had been a whole lot different for me even just a few years later.

Jude sipped from her beer and regarded me.

"I'll think about it," she said after a little while.

We finished the rest of our food in silence, my mind racing with so many questions I still had, but Jude wasn't like an oyster. You couldn't just shuck the truth out in one motion, getting right to the good stuff. Jude was a lobster: a hard outer shell that was difficult to crack that covered squishy insides. No doubt she'd built up that shell for a reason, and it was going to take a damn good reason for her to let someone in.

I didn't know why I was so intent on being that someone, but from the moment I'd seen her getting off that motorcycle, I'd been completely and utterly captivated by her. Maybe it was boredom, but I didn't think so. Sooner or later I was going to figure Jude out. It was probably a better use of my time than moping about my miserable life.

Chapter Four

Jude

I have no fucking clue what made me ask her over. I had promised myself that I wasn't going to talk to her, look at her, interact with her in any way. Yet there she was and my mouth was asking before my brain had decided it was a bad idea. Plus, I did have extra lobsters. My heart had dropped to my feet and I'd begged her mentally to say no, but she didn't. I wasn't going to lie, I was glad that she'd brought the dog with her. I loved dogs and would have one if I wasn't gone so much and wasn't so shitty about taking care of anything.

Iris was funny. Really funny. And sweet, and awkward and... No. I couldn't let myself go there. I didn't even know if she would like me. We hadn't discussed that. At least I hadn't blurted everything out to her, but it hadn't been easy. There was something about Iris that was so open and pure that she made me want to confess all my deepest secrets while I looked deep into eyes that were the color of the ocean when the sun was shining especially bright.

Iris was different enough that she didn't remind me of someone else. Someone else I had loved. No, Iris wasn't like her.

I adored her dog too. Dolly Parton. What a ridiculous name for a dog, but it made complete sense somehow. I could tell Iris was interested in me, interested in why I was back. I had thought about telling her. Considered it, and decided no, definitely not. She'd helped me with the dishes and then had taken the dog and gone back to her parents' house. It had been on the tip of my tongue to ask her to stay. I'd bake a fucking cake or something. I was sure I had something in the cupboards that I could whip up.

I didn't ask her. I let her take Dolly and leave, and then I was alone again, telling myself that I preferred it that way.

A few days later, I was getting ready to go home from the dock when I heard a voice call my name. It was Cindy, who owned The Lobster Pot, the restaurant where most of my lobsters were cooked and eaten. She'd always been fond of me and was a complete sweetheart.

"How are you doing, Jude?" she asked. "How are your folks?"

I didn't feel like making small talk, but I made an exception for Cindy. We chitchatted and I tried to stay down-wind so she wasn't slapped in the face with bait smell.

"Do you want to clean up out back? You can, you know." She'd made this offer before and I'd always declined, but something about today made me say okay. They even had a shower there that I could use, and I had a change of clothes.

I grabbed my extra clothes and followed her toward the rear of the restaurant, and she unlocked the door for me.

"There's shampoo and soap and conditioner in there. Oh, towels." She even had some of those and they were clean and fluffy and smelled like flowers. I didn't know why she was being so sweet to me, but it was throwing me off. I wasn't used to kindness, which was a startling revelation. Although, that was Cindy. One time in high school she'd happened upon me when I'd parked my car in the lot of The Lobster Pot. I'd had a fight with my parents and had needed to leave for a while. I'd fallen asleep and had been woken by her tapping on my window.

She'd made me some coffee, and let me talk, and it had been just what I needed. Strange that I'd forgotten about that until now.

"I hide the key right up here. Use it anytime you want," she said, patting my shoulder and then heading out to the kitchen.

I showered using the hottest water I could get and shampooed my hair twice. I changed into my clothes and felt a thousand times better. Maybe I should do this more often. Then I wouldn't have to strip on the porch and run into the house.

Cindy had even left me a bag for my lobstering clothes. So thoughtful.

I was leaving the shower when I almost bumped into someone wearing jeans, a baseball cap, and the signature red Lobster Pot polo shirt.

"Oh, hey," a familiar voice said and I found myself looking into Iris's blue eyes.

"Hey." Some water from my hair ran down the back of my neck, making me shiver.

"What are you doing here?" she blurted out.

"Just taking a shower," I said, and then realized I had to elaborate because of the confusion on her face. I'd been momentarily distracted by how adorable she looked with her hair in a ponytail coming from the back of the cap.

"Cindy let me. I just got off the boat."

"Oh, yeah? Did you catch a bunch of lobsters?" I didn't want to chat with her, but I didn't want to leave, so I was stuck in a tornado of cognitive dissonance.

"Not bad today." That's what I always said, no matter if it was a good fishing day or a bad fishing day. Most of the fellows in my profession were the strong silent types. Lots of long pauses and then commenting on the weather. Every now and then someone grunted something about a sports team, but that was about it.

"Cool, I bet it's a lot of work," she said, her eyes drifting down to my arms. They'd definitely changed shape since I started hauling traps. I worked out in the off-season to maintain my strength and I'd gotten a little obsessed with weight lifting. Maybe I could put a gym in the basement.

"It is. But, uh, I have to go." I didn't have to go.

"Oh, right. So do I. I was sent back here for...something." She shook her head and her cheeks pinked.

"I should get back to work," she said and I realized that we'd been standing there staring at each other for far too long. Or I'd been staring at her for too long. Definitely that.

"Yeah, I should get home," I said and slid by her in the tight space. I heard her gasp and I hoped it wasn't because I still stunk. That was probably it.

I walked fast toward my motorcycle, refusing to look back to see if she was watching me leave.

When I got back, I saw that my parents had left a message on the home phone. They always did that instead of calling my cell phone. I didn't even know why I still paid for a landline, except that it made the internet bill cheaper. They sounded like they were having a fabulous time, as usual. I knew I needed to call them back, but I was going to have to work up the energy to do that.

I crashed on the couch and took a nap for a few hours, waking up in time to make an early dinner.

Iris and I had eaten all the lobster last night, so I made tacos. I couldn't help but keep looking out the window that gave me a view of their kitchen. Once, I glanced up from chopping lettuce to find her looking at me.

I froze and stared back, like I was caught in a trance. She suddenly turned her head and spoke to someone before glancing once more at me and then giving me a little wave. I waved in return, but I made the mistake of using the hand that was holding a knife. I put it down and tried again. Her lips curved into a smile and then she was gone from the window, probably to have dinner with her parents.

I finished chopping and cooking and sat down to eat. Just as I was rinsing the dishes in the sink, there was a knock at the door, and if I wasn't mistaken, a bark.

I opened the door to find Iris waiting on the other side with a pie.

"I brought pie," she said as Dolly ran into the house and jumped onto the couch.

"What kind?" I asked before I let her in.

"Blueberry."

"You can come in." I stood aside.

"So if I had blackberry, you wouldn't have let me in?" she asked as she followed me toward the kitchen. I had some ice cream in the fridge. You couldn't eat pie without ice cream, as far as I was concerned. That was a crime.

"No, I like blackberry. If you'd had strawberry, I would have thrown you out."

She gasped and set the pie down on the dining table. "What's wrong with strawberry pie?"

"I'm allergic?" I said and went to grab some plates and silverware.

"Oh, well, that makes sense. Sorry about that."

"No worries," I said and we sat down to ice cream and pie as Dolly snored on the couch. Iris had traded her polo for a light blue tee that had a pocket with a kitty face embroidered on it, and she wore a pair of ripped shorts. She was too cute for words. Her damp hair flowed down her back. I wondered if she ever braided it. I had a thing for girls with braids.

"How was work?" I asked to distract myself from memories of another girl with long hair.

She stabbed her fork into a piece of pie as if it had offended her.

"Same old, same old. Only now it's more annoying because I'm older and I don't have a lot of patience for sixteen-year-olds who don't want to do any work and don't really need money and don't give a shit. Teenagers are exhausting." She sighed and shoved a forkful of pie into her mouth.

"I work alone and I like it that way," I said, taking a bite of pie. The bright, rich blueberries burst on my tongue with just a hint of lemon and buttery crust. When I was bitter about my life, there was no one there to tell me to smile. I could even scream at the waves and no one would say a damn thing. It was an ideal situation.

"This is really good. Where did you get it?" I asked. This was even better than the local farm stand's pie, or even the ones from the gas station.

"My mom made it. I'll let her know you liked it. She basically forced me to bring it over to be polite. I mean, I also wanted to pay you back for the lobster last night. So thank you."

"You're welcome."

Dolly came to investigate what we were doing and started begging, but Iris snapped her fingers and told her to go lie down and she went back to the couch in a huff.

"Sorry," Iris said. "She's a good girl and knows not to ask for people food."

"No, it's fine." We lapsed into silence, but I could tell that she didn't like it. She wanted to know things about me that I might or might not want to share.

"How was your day?" she asked as I was scraping the last of the pie off my plate.

"The same," I said, which wasn't a lie. "Most every day is the same. I like it that way."

"Do you go out every day? I feel like I've grown up here but I don't know much about lobstering."

"I do, but I don't fish the same area every day. I had to learn a lot of this stuff the hard way. It just kind of happened. I came home here and I was looking for work and there was a boat and the next thing I knew I was buying it and a pair of rubber pants and painting my own buoys."

I shrugged. Things back then had been a complete blur. I didn't remember much. I'd been too distracted by grief at the time to think logically. I had to hand it to them, the other lobstermen had been really great. Especially Kenny, Boyd, and Travis. I'd been so embarrassed when they'd been kind to me that I'd pulled away and tried to avoid them on the dock. I'd give a wave and pretend like I had somewhere to go when they tried to talk to me. I should probably work on that. They were good guys and I didn't need to be such a bitch all the time.

"Wow, that's really amazing. That you just jumped in like that. I don't do things like that," she said, and the frown on her face told me that she thought it was a bad quality.

"Leaping before you look isn't always the wisest idea." My entire life was proof of that. I was always running head-first without thinking of consequences. True, I lived my life without fear, but it had gotten me into a lot of trouble, and, in my current case, complete and total heartbreak. I'd followed a girl around the US, moving from place to place when we wanted, while she wrote content for websites and I did odd jobs. It had been sheer freedom, being with her. We hadn't needed anyone but each other. Everything about our relationship had been hurling myself into the unknown, from the first day we met by chance in an intro to economics class.

Iris spoke, bringing me back to the present moment. "Oh, I know, but it sounds so gutsy. You ride a motorcycle and are a lobsterman and you live in this house alone and it's all kind of amazing." Her cheeks flushed into the loveliest shade of pink and I had to look away.

She might not think I was so gutsy if she knew the truth, but I was never going to tell her the truth, so it didn't matter. She had made it perfectly clear that she wasn't hanging around and didn't have any plans of staying in Salty Cove. As soon as she got some money together, she would be gone and I'd never see her again, except on holidays. That was how it should be. She was too sweet and vibrant to be stuck in this dull town forever. She could never be happy here. I wasn't happy here, but I wouldn't be happy anywhere so it didn't matter.

"What are you thinking about?" she asked and I wished she would stop wanting to know more about me, but that was the price I paid for having opened the door when she knocked. I mean, I had to pay for the pie somehow.

"This town," I said. Iris made a face and I got up to put the dishes in the sink.

"I can't believe I'm back here. I swore I wouldn't be. I swore I would never live here again, yet here I am," Iris said. She threw her hands in the air and then slapped them down on her legs.

"What were you going to do?" I asked.

"I wanted to do marketing or something for a company that had a good message. That probably sounds idealistic, but that's what I wanted. Want. Still want. But I wasn't the only one who wanted to do that, and I kept getting shut out of jobs. Maybe it wasn't the right dream." She lifted one shoulder and dropped it sadly. "What were you supposed to be doing?"

"I could never make up my mind, but I think I always wanted to be my own boss. Make my own living." I looked down at my hands and turned them over. I'd never had so many calluses in my life. "I got disillusioned in college and changed my mind way too many times, but I think a lot of people do. When they get older and reality sets in."

Silence fell between us.

I expected her to take Dolly and leave, but I found her glancing around the room.

"This is...quite the house," she said. I had a feeling she was referring to the deer head on the living room wall, the plaid couch, and the number of framed pictures of old Moxie soda signs that littered the space. My parents had a very specific decorating style. It wasn't even close to mine, but I still thought of this as their house. I guess I didn't even think about the decor most days. It was extraneous.

"It's hideous. I've always hated it," I admitted, and I could tell that Iris was relieved to hear that I didn't like the interior design either.

"It's awful. Like, truly awful. No offense to your parents," she added.

"I won't tell them you said that." I walked into the living room and sat down next to the sleeping Dolly on the couch. Iris fell into my dad's old chair, which was made of wood and had ugly upholstery with ducks on it.

"Dear god, this chair is uncomfortable," she said, making a face and sitting forward with her arms resting on her legs.

"Sorry about that. We can switch if you want." I looked over at Dolly, who opened one eye and glared at me and then closed it again and went back to sleep, her blocky head resting on her paws.

"No, it's fine. I'm used to Dolly hogging my bed, so why should this be any different. Little greedy monster." She said it in a tone of affection. "I've had her for three years, and sometimes I think that life would be easier without her. Let me tell you, there aren't a ton of people willing to rent an apartment to someone who has a dog. I'm sure other people might have gotten rid of her, but I couldn't. She's my girl. For about five seconds I thought about letting her live with my parents, but I just couldn't be parted from her. We're a package deal."

"You're lucky to have her," I said. I reached over and

started to stroke Dolly's head. Her fur was just a little bit rougher than velvet, and shined in the light. She opened one eye when I touched her ear, but closed it when I went back to stroking her head.

Iris gazed fondly at Dolly and I was a little jealous of the attention.

"I've never had a dog." Not even when I was a kid. My parents would never let me have one. Said I wasn't responsible enough.

"You should get one, but only if you're willing to put in a lot of work. I feel like it's preparing me for kids. If I end up having kids. That's way in the future, after I get back to the city." She glanced out the window and I could tell she was far away.

"Tell me about it," I said, leaning back on the couch. "Tell me about what it was like." I hadn't been out of Maine since I got back. No reason to go anywhere. No place I wanted to visit.

"Make me a cup of tea and I will," she said with a smile that was just a little bit wicked. Or perhaps I just imagined that. I tried not to disturb Dolly as I got up and went to the kitchen to turn on the kettle. I needed something to hold in my hands and a cup of tea was better than anything else.

I waited for the kettle to whistle and added lemon ginger tea bags to two cups.

"Do you want honey or sugar or milk?" I called.

"Just honey please!" she yelled back.

I added the honey to both cups and brought them to the living room.

"Thank you so much," Iris said. She took the mug from me and pulled her feet up on Dad's chair to try and get comfortable. I moved Dolly's feet so I could sit on some part of the couch. When she stretched out her legs, she took up the entire length and then some.

"You can shove her off. She'll grumble, but she'll be absolutely fine," Iris said. "She's spoiled rotten."

I wasn't going to do that to Dolly, so I just kind of shoved her aside and she got all huffy and offended, but went back to sleep in moments. I wish I had her life.

I let Iris have a few sips of tea after it had cooled some before I asked her again.

"Tell me about Boston."

She let out a little laugh. "It wasn't that great. I feel like you're building up your expectations too high. Haven't you ever been there?"

I had, for a brief stay during the Fourth of July a few years ago, but I wasn't going to tell her about that. I pressed my lips together and shook my head. It was a small lie, but small lies pile up and crush you at some point. I'd have to be careful not to stack mine too high.

"Well, it's… Boston, you know? It's all historical shit, and a Dunkin' on every corner and a subway system that sucks, but there's something about it. So different from here." I didn't care what she talked about, as long as she kept talking. Iris was so animated, it was like watching a performer and she didn't even know she was doing it. She'd be great on the stage. I seemed to remember something about her maybe being in the drama club in school. I knew I'd seen her face on a flyer once or twice.

"What else?" I asked. She could tell me the subway schedule. I wouldn't mind. I hadn't had a long conversation with anyone in… I didn't want to think about how long. It was almost a relief to sit here with Iris and let her talk. I hadn't known if it was possible for me to even converse normally with someone I might be attracted to. She seemed comfortable with it, at least I hoped so.

"It's really windy some days. There's no point in doing your hair because it's just going to get blown around. What else? It's ridiculously expensive, which is how I ended up here. I kept having shitty roommates, or my apartments kept getting turned into short-term stays that I couldn't afford. My résumé wasn't impressive enough because I didn't go to Harvard and got average grades and didn't have connected parents to get me an internship. I tried doing one of those while working full time, and it almost killed me. Couldn't get a job in my field without a decent internship because let's make it as easy as possible for the rich kids to stay ahead." She frowned into her mug of tea. I didn't want her to talk about things that made her sad.

"What did you like best about it?"

She sipped and then smiled to herself.

"There was this little hole-in-the-wall Italian place near my apartment. They had the most sporadic hours and weren't open on weekends, except sometimes if you got lucky. It was run by a husband and wife and they were always bickering, but in a cute way. Most amazing hand-

made pasta you've ever had in your life. Pesto made in the
back from basil from the farmer's market. And don't even
get me started on the cannolis. Those things were heaven.
Whenever I would go in there, they would talk to me like
I was a friend and the wife would always give me advice. It
was a little embarrassing sometimes, but I always found it
helpful at some point. I miss that place." She sighed and lay
back against the back of the chair. "And my friends. I miss
them. There was a huge queer community there. Thousands of people would show up for Pride. It was so nice to
be around people who got it. Who knew what your life
was like. We'd have dance parties and bowling nights and
they were always there. Ride or die. I miss them."

Iris sniffed and I thought she might have wiped a few
tears. "I miss the energy and all the people. I miss being
able to put in my earbuds and go to the pharmacy without
someone stopping me to tell me they remember me when
I was in diapers and asking what I'm up to these days." She
mimed gagging and I agreed with her.

Fortunately, I had cultivated a "don't fucking talk to me"
aura since I was young and was rarely approached by anyone
but the bravest of gossipers. It was something I had worked
hard at, but sometimes I wondered if I shouldn't soften my
edges a little. Being hard had worked for me, but where
had it gotten me? I was alone, truly alone, which was what
I wanted, but did I still want that? I didn't know anymore.

"I miss being able to go get something organic without
it being a big deal," she said.

"Hey, Bobby's Market is getting better. I think they

have some organic stuff. They have to for the rich people who come here and are obsessed with Gwyneth Paltrow."

Iris shuddered. Tourists were a necessary evil in a town like Salty Cove. They burst in every summer, trying to change everything and eat all the lobster, and then as soon as it got remotely cold, they were gone again and we were left to our own devices. They were great for the economy, but at what cost? They never wanted to raise taxes to pay for the school, and they didn't care about the snowplow budget, and they took over homes that had been in families for hundreds of years and turned them into architectural nightmares.

"Ew. Well, at least we have her to thank for the ability to buy organic spinach a few minutes away from the house." She finished her tea and set it down on the coffee table with a sigh. "I can't wait to go back. I just need some money and a job. I think I'll be able to find something while I'm here, and just drive down for an interview if I have to. It's going to work out."

She seemed to be just as insistent to convince me as she was to convince herself. I believed her. She was determined, that was for sure. So many people here were only determined to live the same lives as their parents because they'd never experienced anything else outside of that.

"You will," I said to reassure her.

"Thank you. I know I will." Her chin jutted forward, and I experienced a rush of something that might be close to desire, if I let it be. I'd done my best to shut off those parts of myself after everything that had happened. I'd be comfortable if I never had those feelings again. If they withered and died, like an un-watered plant, that would be fine with me.

I shoved aside the feeling and asked her another question about Boston to distract me.

Iris talked and talked. She talked about her apartment, and her college years, and the day she adopted Dolly, and her friends. She told me so many things and I let her. Let her spill it all out into me, because I was so empty. I drank in her stories and her words until I was so full, I wanted her to stop, but didn't tell her to.

"I'm sorry. I'm talking your ear off. You can tell me to leave anytime," she said, pausing and maybe realizing quite some time had passed.

"It's okay. You can talk to me anytime you want."

She looked into her lap and I saw her cheeks flush again. She really was pretty. Her lips were lush and full, as well as her cheeks. Her face was round in all the perfect ways, and those eyes cut right through me. Not to mention her body was full of everything I wanted: roundness and curves and softness. Everything about her was designed to make me want her. I'd never noticed her in high school because I'd been an angry senior, hell-bent on getting the fuck out of here and never coming back. I wasn't going to chase some wide-eyed freshman, no matter how adorable she was. I wouldn't attach myself to anything that would have kept me here, especially not a freshman neighbor. She was too young then, that was for sure, and I'd been so focused on getting out that I'd never really paid attention to her. I wondered if she had changed like I had when I'd left. I wasn't that person anymore. I didn't know who I was.

"I remember you from high school," she said, as if she'd read my thoughts.

"Do you? What do you remember?"

I was morbidly curious about her impressions. I didn't remember a whole lot about high school, only that I wanted it to be over as fast as possible. My parents hadn't supported anything I ever wanted to do, and I'd definitely gotten into my share of trouble. Honestly, I was lucky I hadn't been arrested. It was close. They'd also threatened to kick me out a time or two. My spare time had been spent with trying to learn how to mix drinks because I'd had ambitions to be a traveling bartender. I'd also messed around with cars, and had flirted with the idea of growing weed. Anything that my parents would have hated, that's what I did. It didn't seem as transparent a ploy for attention as it did now.

"I remember you seeming so grown-up and confident. You didn't give a shit what people thought of you. I wanted to be like that." She traced a knot in the arm of the chair with one finger. "I think I envied you a little. I didn't come out until my senior year. Right after prom, actually. Like, buh-bye, fuckers, I'm gay!" That made us both laugh.

"I wasn't," I said. "Confident. I wasn't. And I did care what people thought of me. I cared far too much." That had shifted as I'd gotten older, thank fuck. At this point the caring was buried under so much other shit that I didn't really think about it much. I didn't really care about anything except being left alone.

"Well, you faked it very well. I was struggling with myself at the time and even though I know it wasn't easy, I wanted to be like you."

I didn't want to talk about me. I wanted her to talk more about herself. "When did you know? That you were queer."

"It wasn't until I was like, fourteen?" Iris smiled and shook her head. "And all my friends were obsessed with the idea of getting boyfriends and it made me physically sick to think about. Like, kissing a guy? No fucking way. I even tried it during an ill-fated game of spin the bottle. I also kissed my first girl that night too."

She laughed and the story made me smile a little. Then she continued. "Everyone was egging us on to kiss and I just figured, 'why not?' and I kissed her and it was like everything suddenly made sense. I had a lot of epiphanies that night, but I wasn't really ready to deal with them yet, so it took me a few more years to trust myself enough to know that yes, I liked girls. Loved them. Like, so much."

We both laughed again and it was easy. It was so easy to slide into laugher with Iris. She was an open and inviting person. I hadn't met anyone like her in a long time.

"When did you know?" she asked.

I hesitated for a minute, but then found myself talking. "I feel like I always did, on some level. But it came to a head when I was ten and I had the biggest crush on my best friend at the time, Lacey. She was the prettiest girl in school. Her mom was a hairdresser, so she always had the best braids and the most amazing curls. Her mom would do it every morning and I'd be so excited to get on the bus and see what she'd look like that day. We were so close and I loved her in this really deep way. I know she didn't feel the same, but that didn't stop me from pining and wishing she would at some point. I suffered for a whole year and I didn't even know how to put my feelings into words. I think I tried and she was confused. I was confused too, and it all was just a weird situation. We kind of stopped hanging out after that, and she drifted away and found new friends. A few years later she was dating boys, and I remember watching from afar and being jealous and confused. I didn't get it until I was in high school and then I came out and the rest is history."

I clenched my hands together so she wouldn't see them trembling. I hadn't planned on sharing that much with her, but I'd gotten comfortable and the words just spilled out. I'd left out the part about how my parents reacted, but I bet she already knew about that. It wasn't a huge secret.

"It isn't easy, is it?" she said.

"No." Sometimes it still wasn't.

"Thank you for telling me," she said.

"You're welcome."

Iris yawned. "I should get back to my parents. I'm sure they're wondering why it's taking me so long to deliver a pie." She unfolded from the chair and stood up. Dolly sat right up and whined. "Yes, I'll take you out," she said to Dolly, petting her head before going to the kitchen and putting her mug in the sink. "You can keep the rest of the pie. I already have two in the fridge at my parents'."

I could already picture myself demolishing the rest of it

around two in the morning when I couldn't sleep, so I was grateful she was leaving it with me.

"Thanks," I said.

"Thank you for the tea and the hospitality. I feel like I haven't talked with anyone queer in so long. It's nice."

There were probably other queer people in this town, but I'd isolated myself so much from everyone that I didn't even know where to find them. Maybe she would.

"Same," I said.

"I'll see you later?" she asked. "I mean, I'll probably see you at The Lobster Pot at some point. Um, good luck with the lobstering?" She shuffled toward the door and Dolly whined to leave.

"Thanks." It was on the tip of my tongue to ask her to stay a little longer, but what for? I wasn't going to ask her to spend the night. That would be ridiculous.

"See you later," she said, opening the door, and Dolly bolted down the porch and to the yard next door.

"See you later," I echoed as she shut the door.

The house was so quiet when she was gone, but at least I had pie.

Chapter Five

Iris

Smelling constantly of French fries isn't as glamorous as it sounds. In my first week back at The Lobster Pot, I managed to get three burns, cut my fingers twice, and almost had a meltdown at least four times. The lunch and dinner rushes were no joke, and I hadn't been here in a while. I hadn't seen Jude in almost a week, and it was starting to feel weird.

I'd been distracted with trying to learn the ropes again at work and it was a little rough. Fortunately, Cindy was amazing, and I actually became friends with one of my co-workers, Anya. She was from Germany and had the love-liest accent and would do impressions of her parents to make me laugh. On one particularly bad day, she pulled a lobster out of the tank and pretended to speak as the lobster and give me advice. I'd been crying, but I started to laugh so hard that I cried more. The teen girls we worked with us thought we were complete weirdos. The guy who manned the fryolater never spoke, so he was my second-favorite coworker.

In the rush before lunch, I always found a way to get downstairs near the bathroom with the shower in it. I told myself I was just checking on the supply room across the hall, but I was really looking to see if Jude was there. I didn't see her again after that first day, and I couldn't bring myself to go over to her house again. I didn't want to be a needy weirdo. She was never going to come over to my parents' house, so I just stayed across the yard and caught a few glimpses of her in the house and on her porch.

On Friday night, I saw her drinking a beer and it was like my feet started walking the rest of my body over to the house. Dolly came with me, and I wish I would have thought about bringing something that would give me an excuse. We were out of pie.

"Hey," I said as Dolly made herself comfortable on one of the porch chairs. She was really loving the life here where she could run around as much as she wanted. Dad watched her during the day and they'd totally and completely bonded. I think Dolly loved him more than she loved me. It was going to be a nightmare when I went back to Boston.

"Hey," she said. "Want a beer?"

Why did I feel so awkward when I came over here? She was so intimidating and I was a little in awe of her. Plus, she was hot as fuck. Like, beyond hot. She had everything going for her. The motorcycle, the arms, the mysteriousness, the voice. It was like she was designed to push all my attraction buttons at once. I'd been burned by every girl I'd tried to date, big time. One turned out to be cheating on me, one had literally disappeared never to be heard from again, and one was in jail for laundering money. I didn't know what it was about me, but if there was a bad-girl type, I was bound to be attracted to her.

I was completely and utterly attracted to Jude, and I had no idea what to do about it. She was so far beyond out of my league and why in the hell would someone like her go for someone like me? Plus, I was leaving, so what did it matter anyway?

Jude handed me a beer. I didn't really like it, but I popped the top on the porch railing and drank. It was cold, at least.

"Hey," I said. "I didn't bring pie, but can I still hang out with you?"

Jude narrowed her eyes. "I guess. Just this once. But now you owe me one pie."

"So it's one pie per visit? Is that the toll?"

"No, but it should be."

If I didn't know any better, I would have said that we were flirting.

"I have a new burn to add to my collection." I held up my forearm in the warm yellow porch light. I was going to have plenty of scars to add to the old ones I had from The

Lobster Pot. I guess I would always take this job with me in the future. I'd already sent Natalie pictures of all my injuries and she wrote back that living in Maine was dangerous to my health, which meant I needed to get back to the city.

"You really should be more careful," Jude said, and then she cringed. "Sorry, I sounded like a mom there. I didn't mean to." She kicked her muscled legs up onto the porch railing and I tried not to be jealous of them.

"It's okay." It meant that she cared if I burned myself and that was a little exciting. I couldn't tell if she simply tolerated my presence or was bored or whatever. I mean, I could tell that she didn't have a lot of interaction with other people. I wasn't sure if she wanted it that way or not. My guess was that she did.

Clearly, Jude had something buried deep that she didn't want to talk about. It didn't take a mind reader to see that. She definitely didn't want to tell me about it, but that was okay. I just liked being around her. There was a calm about Jude, a steadiness. After so much chaos in my life recently, it was nice to be with someone like her.

We talked about this and that, nothing serious, nothing deep. Dolly snored and I petted her head. Jude seemed to enjoy Dolly, which was a plus.

"Oh," I said, almost forgetting. "My parents want to invite you for dinner tomorrow. You can totally say no. I already thought up a list of excuses and you can pick the best one." She thought about that for a moment, taking a sip of her beer and staring out into the night as the crickets sang in the tall grass.

"No, it's okay. I see them from time to time. It's not like they're strangers."

I hadn't expected her to say yes. I'd been more prepared for her to say no.

"Really? You want to come over and have dinner with me and my parents?"

"Why not?" She shrugged one muscled shoulder that was on display in her tank top and then did a little shake of her head to get her hair out of her face. I'd seen her do that more than once and it was a little habit that I liked more than I wanted to admit.

Okay. Cool. Now I had to readjust to this new situation. I didn't really want Jude coming over and having dinner with my parents, and I couldn't put my finger on why that made me nervous and squirmy. I wasn't sure if they'd like her, or if she would like them, and I didn't want to be in the middle if things went south.

Since Jude had warmed up to me and there weren't so many silences, I could at least try to keep the conversation going in the right direction.

"My mom is making seafood stew. I hope that's okay. It's really good. I'm also going to attempt to make my dad eat a salad, so stay tuned for how that's going to go." He still refused to eat "food that my food eats," but I think I was making progress. Sure, he wasn't going to be snarfing down kale anytime soon, but we were going to start with romaine and work our way up to spinach. It was a process.

"Sounds challenging."

"Oh, it is."

We sat in silence, listening to the sounds of the night. After a hectic day, there was nothing better than sitting on the porch with Jude while Dolly slept and drinking a beer. Okay, it would be better if I had a sangria, but I wasn't going to tell Jude that. Maybe I'd bring her some next time, in place of the pie. Hopefully she'd take that as payment for my visit.

"What are you doing this weekend?" I asked her. I didn't have any plans other than working a few hours and going to the library with my dad and then getting some groceries. Wild times. I also needed to get some more bedding and a few other things. I'd gone a little wild when I'd moved and had tossed a lot of things after I'd read this organizational book about getting rid of what doesn't bring you joy, and now I needed to buy a bunch of stuff that might not bring joy, but that I actually needed.

"Nothing," Jude said. "There are a few things in the house to be fixed, and I'll mow the lawn and go for a ride, but that's it."

"No getting shitfaced down at the bar and hitting on the local girls?" I asked, trying to tease her.

"Definitely not." She didn't elaborate. I kept trying to draw her out and it was a challenge, but I didn't have anything else to do right now.

"Do you, um, date? Around here?" I knew I was fishing and she knew I was fishing and I didn't care.

"No," she said, and that was that. She pressed her lips together and frowned.

Okay, staying away from that. I didn't want to piss her off

or make her mad or make her not want to see me. Outside of talking to my dad about books and Anya about her life in Germany and dealing with younger coworkers, being with Jude was the best part of my days. Whatever time I wasn't at work or with my parents or Jude was spent on the internet, writing cover letters, tweaking my résumé, looking for potential apartments, and chatting with my Boston friends. They were also on the lookout for opportunities for me, but for right now, I had zero emails in my inbox other than automated ones that I'd already unsubscribed from at least ten times. I'd even looked up some shit about grad school because what I definitely needed was more debt.

Jude interrupted my mental meandering. "Do you date?"

I almost choked on a swallow of beer and burst out laughing.

"I'm sorry," I said, wiping my shirt. Of course I'd spilled. I always did. "Why should I answer you? You didn't answer me." I smirked at her and stared at her mouth a little too long. Her lips weren't very full, but I had the feeling she definitely knew how to use them.

"Dating can be hard," I said. "In general."

"It can be." She still wasn't giving me much. Trying to crack her open was proving to be a difficult job.

"I mean, how do you even know someone else is into you? Do you come out and ask them? Is there a non-weird way to do that? And all of this is further complicated by being a lesbian because how do you know if someone is being friendly or flirty? It's just so confusing." I huffed out a sigh and sat back in my chair and finished my beer. It was warm and I was a little buzzed now.

"It is. I remember when…" She trailed off, as if she'd realized she'd started talking about something she remembered she didn't intend on talking about.

"You remember what?" I said gently. I needed someone to talk to and so did she. Sure, she was the closest person geographically and to my age around here, but there was more to it than that.

"Nothing."

I guess that was the signal that this was over. Her chiseled jaw clenched tight, making her cheekbones stand out. If I didn't know that she was upset, I would have swooned.

"I'll see you tomorrow night," she said, taking my empty beer bottle with her.

"See you tomorrow," I said and whistled for Dolly. It was an abrupt end and I didn't feel great about it, but she'd already gone inside and shut the door. Should I apologize? I wanted to, but I also didn't want to intrude on her privacy, so I stood there for a few moments and then walked down the steps and headed back to my parents' house.

"How was Jude? Is she coming over?" my mom said the second I walked through the door.

"Yeah, she's coming." But I didn't elaborate. Tomorrow might be a complete and utter disaster and I was already sick thinking about it.

"She seems like such a nice girl," my mom said as she put dishes in the dishwasher. Dad was already snoring in his chair, a paperback resting on his chest. Dolly dashed over to her bed and lay down. I needed to get her more exercise. She was becoming a couch potato.

I rolled up my sleeves to help my mom and brought some of the pans from the stove over to the sink.

"She is. But she's quiet. Please don't interrogate her or ask her anything too personal, please?" My mom had a tendency to grill people, but she thought it was in a friendly way so it was okay.

"Oh, hush, it will be fine."

I brought over more dishes and then started wiping down the counters. I wanted to help her out as much as I could with the house, since she worked so hard and Dad couldn't do much.

"I hope so," I said under my breath.

I made Mom some tea after we finished in the kitchen and brought it to her in the living room.

"Do any of your friends from Boston miss you?" she asked.

"Yeah, they keep sending me jobs. A friend's lease is up in a few months, and she's thinking of getting a bigger place, so moving in with her and her other roommate might work. I'll have to get a job first, though."

"Are you sure you want to go back?"

"Of course I do," I said, snapping a little. "Sorry."

She pursed her lips while flipping through the channels and settling on a rerun of *Murder, She Wrote*. She was obsessed with Jessica Fletcher, and rightfully so. I had tried to rope my former roommates into watching it as a marathon, but they'd all declined, so I'd done it by myself. I couldn't wait to live either by myself, or with people who were on my same level. My credit was shit, so getting a place on my own was probably impossible.

"We'll miss you when you go, and I don't think your father and I will be the only ones."

I had the feeling she was talking about Jude. I didn't want to talk about Jude with my mom. It made me feel weird.

"Jude isn't some sort of vegetarian, is she?" My mom said the word *vegetarian* the way some people said *unemployed* or *murderer.* It wasn't a positive thing. I was working on explaining to her that there were millions of vegetarians and even vegans out there. Would probably blow her mind.

"She's not, but even if she was, we would be happy to accommodate her."

My mom made a grumpy sound and stared at the TV. She looked so tired. When I was younger she was always doing something: painting pottery or reading biographies of former presidents or coming up with creative projects for her students. These days it seemed like all she had energy for at night was TV. She'd had to take on teaching English to sixth graders when my dad hurt his back, since just doing real estate wasn't going to cut it anymore. She had a teaching degree and taught before my brother was born, but she'd switched to real estate since it was a little more flexible and had the potential for more money.

"She's allergic to strawberries, though, so you'd better not have any that are anywhere near the food she's going to have."

"I was going to make a berry cobbler and I'll leave out

the strawberries this time. Will change the recipe, but what can you do?"

I gritted my teeth and wanted to tell my mom that Jude didn't invent her allergy to inconvenience us, but that was just a dead-end street. I scrolled on my phone, looking through the social media accounts I followed. One of the designers I loved was doing a new furniture line and I'd been waiting for the reveals so I could fantasize about my dream house. I'd been with my mom enough times when she staged houses to put on the market, and I'd gotten a little hooked on ideas of creating beautiful spaces.

Dad startled awake and his book fell to the floor. "I was just resting my eyes," he said and Mom and I shared a look.

"You've been asleep for two hours," Mom said.

"Preposterous." He leaned down and winced as he picked up his book.

"Nice vocab word, Dad," I said, and he smiled.

"Learning lots of new things from these books." He patted the stack. Mom's eyes were fluttering closed so she would probably be asleep soon.

"Do you want some tea, Dad?" I asked. Mom's was slipping out of her hands, so I took the cup from her and set it on the coffee table.

"Sure, baby girl."

I made him some tea with honey and when I came back, Mom was asleep, tucked into the corner of the couch. I pulled a blanket off the back of the couch and draped it over her.

"She works so hard," Dad said, gazing adoringly at his wife.

"She does," I said. I didn't want to say too much in case she was still kind of awake.

Dad sighed and looked up at me. "It's good to have you back, baby girl."

"It's good to be back," I said. It was true, I loved being here, as long as it was temporary.

Jude's face flashed in my mind and I tried not to think about what she'd be doing in a year. I mean, she had a boat and a house and she'd been here for two years. Didn't seem like she had plans to go anywhere, but I couldn't really understand why she would stay if she was so miserable. She wasn't going to tell me, at least not yet.

"Is Jude going to come over?" Dad said, picking his book back up and flipping the pages to find his place.

"Yes," I said and I told him about her strawberry allergy.

"She's an interesting girl," he said, not looking up from his book. "You two seem to be getting along really well."

If I wasn't mistaken, there was something in his tone that suggested Jude and I might be something other than friends. I didn't even know if we *were* friends. Did drinking beer a few times on someone's porch and sharing lobster rolls and pie a friendship make? I kind of hoped that it did. I wanted to be friends with Jude. I mean, I think I did. Right? I did.

If I was being completely honest with myself, I wanted something else with Jude. Friendship yes, but also...

No, it wasn't going to happen. She was unavailable and

I was leaving. It would never work and it didn't need to. Jude was someone I'd be momentarily close with for a few months and we'd agree to stay in touch, but we never would. We'd nod to each other when I came to visit for Christmas and maybe we'd have tea together with watered-down conversation. We wouldn't talk about anything deep or serious and then we'd go back to our lives. Hell, maybe she'd get on her motorcycle one day and this town would never see her again.

"She's cool," I said to my dad in what I hoped was a noncommittal tone. I didn't want to get their hopes up on anything. If I wasn't careful, they'd start envisioning me living next door for the rest of my life so they could play with grandkids every day.

He shook his head. "It will be nice to get to know her a little better. There aren't a whole lot of women who could handle that job, hauling those traps."

"Right?"

I didn't have the upper body strength for that, and I didn't think I could stick my hands (even in gloves) into a barrel of old fish guts and re-bait the traps. No, thank you.

"I'm going to bed after I take Dolly out," I said. It was absurdly early for me to go to sleep, but I wanted to sit in my room and fuck around on my computer or watch a movie by myself for a little while. It was hard to get alone time these days. My dad was always around during the day and my mom was always wanting to chat, and then there was work, and I missed the anonymity of the city. I was going to use that to fuel my desire to get back to Boston. I wouldn't have to worry about my mom catching me masturbating. I couldn't go through that again. It was a wonder we survived the embarrassment from last time.

I let Dolly into the yard and grabbed her ball so she wouldn't sprint to Jude's porch and then I'd have to run and get her. The lights were still on at Jude's place, but I didn't want to bother her. She'd probably had enough of me already. I hadn't had enough of her yet, not even close. That realization shook me and I tried not to analyze it too much. Nothing was going to keep me from getting back to the city that I loved.

Dolly raced after the ball I threw as if she was having the time of her life. I hummed "Jolene" while I threw it and tried to decide what kind of reading mood I was in tonight. I rotated through books frequently. Right now I was flipping between a nonfiction about the history of salt, a historical romance set during slavery, and a young adult fantasy that Dad had just finished about magical storms.

I was still deciding when I heard a door open and close. I glanced over my shoulder and saw Jude leaning against the railing of the porch, her dark hair kind of flopped in her face. She did that little flip of her head, tossing it back, as if she'd designed the gesture to draw attention to her incredible cheekbones and turn me on in the same breath. Why did she have to be so attractive? The fact that she was taller than me just made it even worse.

"Hey," I said because it would have been rude to stare at her without speaking.

"Hey," she said back. We needed to come up with a less-awkward greeting. "You want to throw the ball?" As soon as the words left my mouth, I wanted a hole to open up in the yard and swallow me whole. Jude probably thought I was a huge dork and didn't want to come over for dinner with my parents anymore. My mom would ask questions and I'd have to explain and then I would have no one to talk to about anything. It would be a completely awful experience every time I came home and had to avoid bumping into her.

"Yeah, sure," Jude said, stopping the runaway train of my thoughts. I tended to do that: imagine the worst-case scenario right off the bat. Although, I hadn't predicted having to live with my parents in the town I'd done everything to escape. Nope, that one had been a surprise.

Jude walked down the steps and over to me. Dolly frolicked and I could tell she wanted to jump on Jude, but she knew that Jude was an alpha. I knew it too.

"Sorry, it's a little slobbery," I said, passing her the damp tennis ball. She took it without hesitation. I tried to keep my eyes on her face and not on her outfit. This time it was a black tank with the same shorts. Her arms really were spectacular.

Jude chucked the ball down the driveway and Dolly took off at warp speed to chase it.

"Wow," I said involuntarily. "Did you play softball? I can't remember."

Jude shook her head. "No, I just haul a lot of traps. I lift weights in between to keep my arms strong."

I could tell. Her thigh muscles bulged from under the

shorts and I had to lift my eyes to her face again. Even that didn't help because every single angle of her was incredible.

"Do your parents like wine?" she asked.

"What?"

Dolly dropped the ball and Jude let it fly again.

"I'm only asking because I want to bring something with me when I come to dinner and wanted to know if they liked wine. I can pick some up before I come over."

"They're more beer people, but if you wanted to get something a little fancier from, like, Portland or something, that would be cool. They drink too much crappy beer." I shuddered. I would be happier with a glass of something pink and sparkling.

"What would *you* like me to bring?" Jude asked, as if she'd read my mind.

"Beer is fine."

"That's not what I asked," she said with the tiniest of smiles. Or I might have just imagined it in the dim light. I liked seeing her smile.

"I like alcohol that doesn't taste like alcohol. Something fizzy that's sweet and tastes like berries is the best. Not strawberries, though, for you."

Dolly started just running in circles in the yard, ball forgotten. She was going to crash in just a few minutes. I needed to do this more with her. When I'd been in Boston I'd had a dog-walker during the day when I was at work. I hadn't had the money to pay her, but I'd found it because I wanted Dolly to have a good life.

"I'll see what I can find," Jude said, and I felt myself

blushing, even though it wasn't really something to blush about. She was just being nice.

Jude looked out at the driveway and then inhaled through her nose. "I should get to bed. I have to be up in a few hours."

Shit, that was right. She had to get up before the sun to be out on a boat. I couldn't imagine. As had become our pattern, we didn't know how to end our interactions. I knew I didn't want to say goodbye, but something had to be said, and we seemed to resort to the most simple of words.

"Yeah, of course. I'll see you tomorrow night?"

"See you tomorrow night," she said before turning and walking back toward her house. I tried not to watch her ass as she walked up the stairs.

I failed miserably.

Chapter Six

Jude

I tried not to be nervous as I knocked on the front door, bottle of sparkling whatever in one hand. I'd found the cutest bottle in the sparkling wine section of the grocery store, hoping that Iris would like it.

"Come in, come in," Iris's mother, Sarah, said. I'd known her over the years and always liked her. She didn't look much like her daughter, but when she smiled, I saw Iris's smile. Guess there was a resemblance.

"Hey," Iris said, coming up behind her mom.

I held the bottle of wine out in front of me. "This is for you." It wasn't much. Maybe I should have also brought flowers or something else.

"This is lovely, thank you," Sarah said, taking the wine from me.

Iris snatched the bottle from her mother. "Ohhh, this is my favorite kind. How did you know?"

"I guessed," I said and heard someone clearing their throat in another room.

"Yes, yes, we're coming," Sarah said, rolling eyes that were the exact same shade of blue as Iris's. "We're coming, Kevin."

Iris gave me a look and I followed the two of them into the house and toward the living room. There, seated in a reclining chair was Kevin, Iris's father. I knew he had hurt his back and didn't see him out and about as much. He had a large stack of books next to his chair and a lamp lit beside him.

"Is that Jude Wicks?" he said, and used both arms to push himself to a standing position. Sarah rushed over, but he waved her off.

"I'm fine, don't fuss." Kevin walked over to me and put his hand out. "It's been a long time since I saw your folks. How are they doing?"

I shook his meaty hand with mine and waited for him to get settled back into his chair. "They're good," I said, which was as much as I knew. I guess they'd agreed that I was grown now and didn't need them as parents anymore and it was their time to live, so we didn't speak that often. It was fine, but sometimes I wished they cared a little more. They didn't know why I'd come back here, but at least they'd let me have the house rent-free since it was paid off. They knew I'd been in a long-term relationship, but I simply told them that it had ended, not how. We always kept our conversations on the surface. I had tried to let them in on my life too many times, but they had never listened, so I'd stopped trying. It was easier to just not tell them anything at all.

"I wouldn't mind moving down to Florida myself. Then I wouldn't have to deal with these damn winters anymore," Kevin said with a laugh. "You ever go down and visit?"

"Yeah, I'm thinking about spending Christmas down there," I lied. I'd gone down to see them the past two years, and I couldn't do it again this year. They'd dragged me out to their friends' parties and I didn't want to have to answer a million inane questions from people I didn't know or care about again.

Kevin grumbled to Sarah about living in Florida and I stood there awkwardly until she turned her attention to me.

"So sorry, Jude, can we get you anything? We could pop that bottle of wine."

"Sounds good. Can I help with anything?"

Sarah waved me off and told me to get comfortable. Iris looked at her mother as if she wasn't sure what to do. I nodded at her and she scurried behind her mother to the kitchen after flashing me a quick smile. Dolly came over and put her head in my lap and whined for attention.

"You are such a beautiful girl, yes you are," I said, stroking her velvet forehead. Her eyes were such a brilliant shade of light blue, they didn't seem real.

"You read, Jude?" Kevin asked.

"Uh, yeah. When I'm not exhausted," I said. I was a fan of cozy mysteries and nonfiction about strange things, and every now and then I threw myself into an epic fantasy that was big enough to be used as a doorstop. I was all over the map, really.

"You should read this one," he said, pulling a book out from the stack that teetered and nearly fell over before he got the right one.

I looked at the cover and then read the back and was surprised. It was queer as far as I could tell. Maybe Iris had given it to him. I knew my father wouldn't read something like that, even if he was supportive of me personally.

"Looks good," I said. It really did.

"You read it and tell me how it is. I just renewed it from the library so you have two weeks. If you need longer, let me know." He started chatting about the other books he was reading, and I'd never seen a grown man so excited about books in my life. He burned through so many that I wondered how the library was able to accommodate him.

Iris and Sarah came back with wine for everyone and glasses of water.

"Dinner will be ready in about ten minutes, so you can just chill in here," Sarah said. "Iris, can you set the table?"

I could tell Iris didn't want to, but she got up and did it anyway. Kevin told me more about his favorite books as I petted Dolly and I wasn't having a horrible time. I hadn't known what to expect when I came over, but I was already glad that I had. Iris's parents were warm and inviting, and I couldn't remember the last time someone had cooked me dinner.

"Okay, come and get it," Sarah called.

I wanted to offer to help Kevin out of his chair, but I didn't and he hefted himself up and we headed to the dining room. There were several cushions on his chair to support his back and he sank down into them with a sigh.

The plates were mismatched, but they had all kinds of different flowers on them. I sipped my wine as Sarah dished out seafood stew into large bowls that had blue lobsters painted on the sides. The steam rose and brought with it the aroma of cream and lobster, shrimp and fish. And butter. Lots and lots of butter.

I grabbed my spoon and loaded it up before blowing on it a few times to cool things down. My eyes closed and I savored one of the most incredible things I'd ever put in my mouth.

"This is fabulous," I said through a mouthful.

"Thank you. It's a family recipe."

"I'd love to get it." I definitely wasn't going to be able to recreate this, but I wanted to have fun trying.

"She won't even give it to *me*," Iris said, glaring at her mom. "I literally stood there and watched her make it and I couldn't tell you what's in it. I should probably pay better attention next time."

"You'll get that recipe when I die. It's printed out in my safety deposit box, along with my grandmother's pearls and a few other things." Wow, that recipe was serious business.

"Can you please not talk about dying right now?" Iris said.

"Yes, let's talk about a more positive subject," Kevin said. "We don't want Jude to think we're a bunch of morbid people."

I wouldn't have minded. I was a morbid person. Or at least I was now. Life had made me morbid.

"Okay, then you make a suggestion," Sarah said, snapping a little. Iris and I shared a look and she shrugged a little apology.

"Jude, cake or pie?" he said, firing the question at me.

"Uh, both?" I said after a few seconds. "Depends on my mood."

"Definitely pie," Iris said. "Unless it's Funfetti. Then cake."

"Pie is right and cake is wrong," Sarah said and we all went around the table, talking about our favorite cakes and pies and other desserts before moving on to other food. After that it was talking about people we knew in town. Sarah knew everyone's shit. Apparently teachers-slash-real-estate-agents had all the gossip. I made a note to not get on her bad side. She also had a memory like a steel trap and could tell you who had a feud with whom from thirty years ago.

By the time we made it to dessert, a mixed berry crumble, I had laughed and I was a little buzzed on the sparking wine and I couldn't remember the last time I'd felt this relaxed. It scared me because relaxing meant that I might slip and say something I didn't want to say, or share something I didn't want to share. I had to be on my guard, always.

I was always one memory away from a breakdown, and I couldn't let that happen in front of anyone else.

We all had coffee and then went back to the living room. Iris did the dishes, so I sat and talked crocheting with Sarah as Dolly tried to climb into my lap. Sarah said she had some old yarn and hooks that she'd bought a while ago and never had time to use, so I was leaving with a full belly and a bag of new yarn to play with.

All in all, a nice evening. Kevin started yawning and I could tell that they wanted to go to bed. I thanked them for everything and accepted the container full of cobbler that Sarah pushed into my arms, along with the crochet supplies.

"I'll walk you back over?" Iris said. I could tell she wanted to know what I thought of her parents and if I'd ever want to talk to her again.

"Sorry about them," she said after she closed the front door and we walked down the stairs together. Dolly was still asleep inside.

"Sorry for what?"

"They're just…parents." She shrugged.

"Yeah, they are, but they were nice. Your dad is really cute."

She laughed. "He's much more interesting to talk to now that he's reading and isn't busting his ass and his back at that job anymore. He was really tired and bitter for a long time. I had so much fucking guilt for being in Boston when he was hurting. I was coming back almost every weekend, putting miles on my car and trying to help Mom out. My grades started slipping, so I ended up on academic probation. I've never told anyone that. My parents didn't know. I got my shit together to graduate, but I wasn't getting any academic honors."

I'd had no idea about any of it. I'd been long gone and my parents hadn't said anything during our infrequent phone calls. That must have been a rough time for all of them.

"That's too bad," I said. "When did he hurt his back?"

We reached my porch and I sat down on the steps with the cobbler in my lap.

"A few years ago during a snowstorm when the power crews were out for like three days straight. He'd pulled it earlier, but then he just overdid it and the damage was permanent. He's had surgery, which has helped, but it will never completely heal. He's in pain a lot. I don't know what to do to help him, you know? He says he doesn't want help, but he needs help, but I don't know how to help. It's a mess. I'm still trying to figure it out."

"I'm sorry. That sounds hard for everyone involved."

"My mom is struggling and I don't know how to help her either. I feel awful for leaving and wanting to go back, because they really need me here, but what about me? What about what I want? I can't have what I want if I stay here. I mean, The Lobster Pot isn't open all year-round and I don't have a lot of other skills that I'd need to get a good paying job. What would I do here?" She looked around as if the answer was going to present itself in the yard.

"I only have a job because I bought a boat in a fit of… something. I don't even remember, really. I was in a haze."

"From what?" she asked and I shook my head.

"Nope, not ready," I said.

Iris sighed. "That's okay. Maybe you'll tell me someday."

Our eyes met and we both stopped breathing for a second and the only sound I could hear was the beating of my heart and the crickets chirping.

I blinked and she leaned forward a little. I don't think she knew she was doing it. If I let myself, I could have kissed her. The worst part wasn't that I could have. The worst part was that I *wanted* to.

I wasn't going to kiss her, so I tore my gaze away from her face and looked down at the glass container in my lap. It was still slightly warm.

"I should probably go inside," I said.

"Oh, right. I'm sure you have to get up early."

I did, but that didn't really matter.

"Thank your parents for everything and tell them I had a lovely time." I stood and she faced me. The hurt in her eyes was naked, raw. I couldn't keep standing here with her like this.

"I will," she said, and stepped off the porch.

"I'll see you later."

"See you," she said over her shoulder.

Part of me ached to call her back, but I couldn't. If I called her back, I was going to kiss her and I couldn't kiss her. I couldn't kiss anyone. I had fully prepared myself for a life of solitude. Love had chewed me up and spit me out. I'd gambled and lost everything to someone else.

"Oh, Grace. I miss you."

I looked up at the sky. It was late, but the sun was still stubbornly waiting to set. I wiped a few tears from my cheeks. No crying. I couldn't let myself start to cry or I'd never be able to stop.

I exhaled when I heard the door slam to the house next door and I knew Iris was inside and safe.

Chapter Seven

Iris

On the whole, the night had gone pretty well, except for a tiny bit of parental bickering and nagging Jude with questions. I shouldn't have gone over to her place. I should have just said goodbye when she'd left the house and called it good. But no, I had to walk her back to her house and there was a moment, and the rejection was clear. I hadn't even meant to lean into her, to show her how I felt, but it happened and now I was just a tiny bit crushed.

To anyone looking in from the outside, it was insignificant. To me, it was as if she'd thrown cold water on me.

Jude definitely didn't want to kiss me, which was fine. That was her right. It made things a little difficult since I wanted to kiss her more than I'd wanted to kiss anyone in my whole life. I wanted to kiss Jude more than I wanted… well, just about anything. Not more than I wanted to leave Maine, that was for sure, but I wasn't comfortable with how close those two were in the race for what I wanted.

I wanted to kiss Jude and know Jude and be with Jude. It would be silly to deny that anymore. I couldn't chalk it up to just being bored. I wouldn't feel this strongly from boredom alone. No, there were so many things about Jude that were intriguing and fascinating and perplexing and frustrating and arousing.

I wanted to know everything about her. I wanted to know her opinions on everything. I wanted to know what her first thoughts were when she woke up before the sun. I wanted to know what she thought about while she was hauling traps. I also wanted to know what her hair looked like when she woke up. I wanted to know what she wore to bed, if anything. I wanted to categorize her smiles. I wanted to memorize her freckles. I wanted to know what her lips tasted like.

That was never going to happen, so I was in for a rough road of pining. Once I got out of here and wasn't seeing her every day, it would get easier. Once I was back in Boston, I'd forget and meet someone new.

When I got back to the house after that little interlude with Jude, my mom was reading a book with the TV on and Dad had gone to bed.

"So, what's the verdict?" Mom said, not looking up from her paperback.

"Verdict on what?"

"Verdict on us. Do you think she'll be willing to have dinner with us another time?"

I sat down on the couch next to her and Dolly jumped up to loaf between us. "Why are you so eager to get her over here, anyway?"

"Because she's alone and it's hard to be alone. Because her parents are in Florida and I happen to know she doesn't get along that well with them. Because it's the neighborly thing to do." Well, when she put it that way, it made sense. I should have figured that out. "It's really kind of you to go over there and befriend her. I haven't said this, but I'm proud of you for that."

I wasn't going to tell her that part of the reason I was being so nice to Jude was because I was completely attracted to her. It wasn't completely out of the goodness of my heart; I wasn't that saintly. More horny than anything right now.

"Thanks," I said because I wasn't explaining my horniness to my mom. Not now, not ever.

"She's a good girl. Works hard. I think about her a lot, being by herself over there. I know she doesn't go out, probably because she's so tired from hauling traps, but still. I worry about her. I thought about bringing her something, but I didn't want to impose. I also didn't want to seem like I was trying to mother her."

I snorted. "Mom, you mother everyone whether they want it or not."

She glared at me and returned to her book. "I don't mother *everyone*."

I was going to let that slide because I was tired from the wine and didn't want to argue. It was sweet that she cared so much about Jude. I wondered what Jude was doing right now. Was she watching TV and reading a book? Was she already asleep? Was she trying to sleep and staring at the ceiling instead? Was she thinking about me?

I said good-night to my mom and went to bed. My body was tired, but my mind was restless, thinking too much about Jude. This was starting to feel like a crush, or maybe I was already there and just in denial.

"What am I going to do, Dolly?" I asked.

What if I couldn't save up enough money or get an apartment or get a job all at the same time? I had to have those three things in place before I went or I was just going to end up back here. I was sending out résumés and cover letters and all that shit and all I'd gotten were three rejections and silence. I wasn't what they were looking for. What a huge blow to my ego. I'd even tried applying to jobs I didn't have much experience for, hoping that maybe confidence would be appreciated, but so far, no good.

As far as saving money, I was doing well on that front. I'd cut off all my nonessential spending, if I'd ever had any, and my parents weren't charging me rent, so nearly all of my paycheck went right into my savings account, or to pay off my credit card bills.

My money thoughts were interrupted by more Jude thoughts, which were far more interesting and distracting.

The crush-like feelings were there in the morning, but I didn't have the benefit of work to distract me. I was hanging out with my dad. He could still drive, but it made both my mom and I nervous, so I was his chauffer, with Dolly sticking her head out the back window, ears flapping and eyes closed in bliss.

She was allowed to go into the library with me, thanks to the fact that they allowed dogs. Dolly scampered around me as I carried a stack of books to return.

"Hello, Gladys," Dad said to the librarian who rushed over to help me with the books. She took them from me with more strength than I thought she would have.

"Hello, Kevin, how are you? A bunch of your holds are in, do you want to pick them up?"

Dad's eyes lit up and Gladys brought out another pile of books. I ended up taking those to the car, and then Dad said he wanted to browse. I left him to his own devices as I walked around with Dolly. I might as well get some stuff while I was here. I headed to nonfic first and found a few things that interested me, including a few true crime books, a book about poisons, and one about a dead president, before going to the general fiction. I found Dad in the young adult section.

"Dad, this is too many books."

He looked up at me as if I'd said the dirtiest curse word. "There is no such thing as too many books."

I started to argue, but whatever. This was bringing him joy and lifting him up, so I should just shut up and let him have as many books as he wanted if it was making him happy.

"Want me to check these out for you?" I asked.

"Sure. I'm just getting through. Can you help me with the top shelf?" I was shocked that he had asked. My dad was not a man that asked for help, but I could see that his back was hurting him.

"Absolutely," I said. "Be right back." I left Dolly with him and she curled up and shut her eyes.

I went to check the books out with Gladys, the librarian. She seemed to be a fixture in my dad's life, but she hadn't been the librarian when I was younger, so I didn't know her.

"You're Iris, aren't you?" she said, scanning my books.

"I am."

She gave me a bright smile that made almost her entire face wrinkle. She had to be at least seventy, or maybe older, with pure white hair twisted into a jeweled clip.

"Your father is one of our best customers. I love it when he comes in. And did I see a doggie with you?" She pushed the stack of books back at me with fingers that were heavy with silver rings.

"Yes, that's Dolly. I can bring her over if you'd like to say hello." Dolly was such a friendly dog that she loved getting to meet new people. I'd worked hard on her manners so she didn't jump or startle anyone when we were out in public.

I went back and took her leash, leading her back to the counter. Gladys came around and leaned down.

"Hello, gorgeous," she said, petting under Dolly's chin. Dolly lapped up the attention as if she'd never been petted in her life.

"My wife's family used to raise show dogs." The word

wife wasn't lost on me. Oh. So Jude and I weren't the only queers in Salty Cove.

"What kind of dogs?" I said, squatting down to be at her eye level.

Gladys and I ended up both sitting on the floor of the library, petting Dolly and talking about dogs. I wanted to tell her I was queer too, but there wasn't a good place to slip it in, so I just held the information and hoped that she would recognize that I was like her.

"Are you settling in okay, with being back?" She stood up and winced, rubbing her lower back.

"I mean, kind of. I'm working at The Lobster Pot, but nothing else other than that."

"You know, we have a lot of clubs and groups that meet here. Maybe one of them would be good for you?" She took me over to the message board at the entrance where there were flyers for upcoming library activities, lost cats, and local business advertisements.

Someone called Gladys back to the desk.

"If you have any questions, come find me. It was nice to finally meet the famous Iris. Your father talks about you all the time." She squeezed my arm and left me to look at the board.

There were all kinds of groups meeting, but one that caught my eye.

There was a queer club. A group that met at the library for cookies and conversation, according to the description. My mouth dropped open and I took a picture of the flyer with my phone so I wouldn't forget.

I fetched Dad and then we spent the rest of the day getting lunch and hanging out. We stopped to get a few things at the store, and bought Jude some beer. Jude's motorcycle was in the driveway when we got home, so I knew she was around. I dropped Dolly off with Dad and took a deep breath before I walked up the stairs to the porch and knocked on her door. It took a few moments for her to answer.

"Hey," I said, and I could hear the nervousness in my voice.

"Hey," she said, her hair damp. She had a towel around her neck, as if she'd just come from the shower. I didn't need to think about Jude in the shower, so I closed my eyes and then held out the little bag to her.

"It's not pie, but will this work? Someone gave it to me at work, and I thought you might like it." As soon as I said it, I realized that my plan was ridiculous. She was going to see right through it. A mastermind, I was not.

"Oh," Jude said, startled. She opened the bag and pulled out the bottle opener and smiled.

"This is cute, thank you," she said. "Do you want to come in?"

Hell yes, I wanted to come in, but I was trying to be cool. "Yeah, sure. If you're not busy."

"No, I'm not busy." She rubbed the towel on her head and it made her hair stick up everywhere. Why was she so damn attractive? It was really irritating.

"Good haul today?" I asked as she went to the kitchen and stuck the bottle opener onto the fridge.

"Not bad. I'm tired, though," she said with a yawn. Oh. That meant I probably needed to leave pretty quick.

"I can go, if you want to sleep," I said, starting to back up.

"No, no. It's fine. I'm used to being exhausted." That didn't sound good, but I kept my mouth shut. She didn't need me telling her what she probably already knew.

"How's your dad?" she asked as we sat in the living room. I had to keep reminding myself not to stare at her body. It was those damn shorts and those damn tank tops. They hugged her body as if they were in love with it. It seemed impossible that someone could look so good in something so simple.

"He's good. Took him to the library today so he's a happy camper. I'm going to take Dolly to the beach after it closes for the night so she can take a swim. Do you want to come?" I wasn't sure who was more shocked by what I said, me or Jude. I definitely had not intended to invite her to come walk my dog. What was I even doing?

"Uh, okay," she said, after a little hesitation. We both seemed bewildered by this conversation, but I guess we were going to the beach.

"Great. I think I'm going after dinner. Is that too late for you?"

She yawned and shook her head. "I'll take a short nap here in a minute."

"Okay, I'll let you do that. I think I'm going to make dinner for my parents, so I should get that started. I'll, uh, see you soon." I left so quick it was like I'd committed a crime. I didn't even hear Jude say goodbye.

I made salmon with asparagus and sweet potato fries for dinner and to my surprise, my parents devoured it. Success! I grabbed my keys and Dolly's ball and was headed out the door.

"I'm taking Dolly to the beach," I said, not mentioning Jude.

"You should invite Jude," my mom called from the kitchen.

"See you later," I called back as if I hadn't heard her.

I put Dolly in the car and knocked on Jude's door.

It was a cool evening so she'd put on a pair of gray sweatpants and a black shirt. Cruel. It was cruel how good she looked.

"You ready?" I asked.

She did look a little more refreshed than she had earlier. "Yeah," she said.

Our only interactions so far had been in either of our houses and at The Lobster Pot. Being in the car with her was going to be something else entirely. We'd be sharing the same air in a confined space. Dolly was our chaperone, but she wasn't much of one because she was too busy sticking her head out the window.

I backed out of the driveway so slowly that she probably thought it was the first time I'd driven a car. I got out on the road and didn't know what to say. The beach was only a seven-minute drive, but seven minutes could feel like forever if someone didn't say something.

"Do you go to the beach a lot?" Jude asked. I glanced over and she was twisting her fingers together in her lap. I wondered if she was nervous too.

"Yeah, I used to, all the time. Mom would pick me up from school and we'd go, and just about every day I'd go during the summer. I need to get back to going while I'm here. The beaches near Boston are crowded and expensive and not nearly as nice. I can't remember the last time I swam in the ocean." That water was brutally cold, but as a kid, I hadn't minded as much. Now it would probably take me a lot to get all the way in.

"Me neither," Jude said. "I know how to swim, of course, but I'm on the water every day, never in it." I turned my head and saw she had a smile on her face so I laughed.

"We should challenge each other. I think I'd be much more likely to stick to something if I had a buddy."

I cringed at calling Jude a buddy.

"I think we could try that," she said. "I don't think it's warm enough tonight, though. And I didn't bring anything to swim in."

It was on the tip of my tongue to suggest skinny-dipping, but I was able to hold it back. Too close, though. Too close. I was going to have to be more careful that I didn't let something like that slip.

"Next time," I managed to say. I waited for Jude to object, but she didn't. Well, that was something. We would have a future swimming excursion. At this point, we'd only hung out at one of our houses, so this was progress.

We made it to the beach without incident. The gate to the beach parking lot was closed, so I just put the car on the side of the road. There were two other vehicles, which wasn't a surprise. Lots of other people enjoyed a nighttime walk in the sand. During the day, the sand was dotted with towels and umbrellas and coolers filled with drinks and sandwiches. Children competed with the seagulls to see who could scream the loudest. Every now and then an older man with a metal detector would lumber by, looking for lost quarters. On times when the tide was high, there would be less sand space, so everyone would be crammed together and if you didn't like overhearing everyone else's conversations, you were in for a rude awakening.

The beach was best at night when the sand was cool and the ocean glowed from the light of the moon.

I kept Dolly on her leash at first, so we could make sure there weren't any other dogs that she might chase. She was usually pretty good, but you never knew.

Jude and I walked through the parking lot with Dolly, and I asked her if she'd made any progress with the yarn my mom had given her. I didn't know about the crochet-ing, and it didn't seem like something Jude would do, but I was interested to see what she made.

"I'm working on a blanket right now, and I'm going to use some of it to fill in a few squares. I also found this re-ally cute pattern for a hat that I'm going to make for winter." I wanted to ask her if she'd make me a hat, but that was a little presumptuous.

"I need a new hobby," I said. Living in Boston was a hobby in itself, but now that I wasn't there, I needed something to do with my extra time until I went back. The only thing I did that could be remotely considered an interest was looking through interior design sites and social media accounts. I loved imagining my dream Boston apartment or even my dream home. I just didn't have the money right now, but when I did? I would have that freaking shiplap on the walls.

We reached where the dirt of the parking lot met the start of the sand. I leaned down and took off my shoes and socks, squishing my toes in the cool sand. Jude did the same and we hid our shoes by the trashcan so no one could take them.

"What about…embroidery?" Jude suggested.

"No, I don't think my fingers are that coordinated."

"How about baking?"

"Maybe. It seems so complicated though."

"What about acting? Weren't you in drama club?"

"I don't know if I want to commit to that. Do you have any idea how much work it is to put on a play? And you don't even get paid for it."

Jude and I chatted about other potential hobbies as we squished our toes in the sand.

"That feels really good," Jude said with a sigh. Dolly was eager to tromp around, so we walked forward and I scanned the beach up and down and saw a few people but no other dogs. I unclipped the leash from her collar and let her prance around. She was completely pleased with herself, her tongue lolling out of her mouth as she galloped up and down the beach and searched for the perfect stick for us to throw.

"She's such a goof," I said.

"Some lobstermen have dogs on their boats, but I think I'd worry too much and get distracted from work."

"Do you ever worry being out there by yourself?" I asked.

"I mean, not really? I probably should worry more." That was unsettling and I didn't really want to pursue it so I changed the subject.

"Want to see how cold the water is?" I asked.

"Sure."

We walked from the drier sand at the edge of the beach down toward where the waves lashed at the shore. The tide was about halfway out or in, depending on where it was going. I bet Jude knew.

The moment the water hit my toes, I gasped.

"Oh, shit, that is icy," I said, looking at her, but she just walked right in up to her ankles and looked back at me.

"Doesn't feel that bad to me."

"Are you part polar bear?"

She shuffled her feet in the water and then walked until she was almost up to her knees. "Maybe," she said with a little laugh.

She looked out to the endless waves and there was so much longing in her face that it caused a lump in my throat, and I had to blink my eyes a few times not to cry. There was a deep sadness in Jude that scared me. I didn't know what caused it, but I did know that you couldn't heal from something like that overnight.

You couldn't ignore it and wish it would go away either.

Dolly came gallivanting over to us, splashing without a care in the world. I was doused in the completely freezing water.

"Thanks, Dolly. That was just what I needed."

I heard a sound while I was wiping stinging salt water from my eyes and when I could see again, I found Jude laughing at me.

I loved the sound of her laugh. It was a thick, rich sound, like warm smoked honey. It sent shivers down my spine, and I knew I would do anything in the world to hear that sound just one more time.

"Sorry," she said, but she didn't look sorry at all.

Dolly came over and sat in the water and looked up at me as if she was extremely pleased with herself.

"You got your mama wet," Jude said. "Are you happy now?" Dolly wagged her tail in the water, splashing me again, and made a whuffing noise. "You want me to throw your ball?"

At the sound of the word *ball* she barked and jumped up and down.

"Now you've done it," I said as I pulled the tennis ball out of my pocket. I handed it to Jude. "You can throw it further."

Jude reeled her arm back and chucked the ball across the

beach, aiming right for where the waves met the shore. Dolly raced after it.

"I'm guessing she's going to love you more than she loves me here pretty soon," I said.

"No, she'll always love you more."

"I hope so, because that would be really depressing if she didn't."

We started walking again, and my feet were completely numb. It was weird to walk out of the water again. The breeze was colder on my wet skin.

"I think I need a new bed," she said. "I'm still sleeping on the same one I had in high school."

I shuddered. That could not be good for her back. "You have got to get a new bed. Like, tomorrow. Do you have to go fishing tomorrow?"

She shook her head. "No. I usually only go out five or six days a week. I change what day I take off, but I was planning on taking tomorrow off anyway."

"Okay, we are going mattress shopping. What's your bed frame situation?"

"I mean, the mattress is on a frame. If you're asking if I have a headboard, the answer is no."

I made a disgusted sound and shook my head. "We're getting you a bed."

Jude started to protest, but I stopped her.

"I need to look at beds too," I said, "so this isn't completely altruistic. Come on, you know you want a new bed. Doesn't your body want a new bed?" I shouldn't talk about her body because it made me think about her body.

Jude rolled her eyes a little and I was relieved to see more of her personality coming out the longer she was with me. It just made my attraction to her stronger, which was a serious problem.

"If you insist," she said.

"I do. I very much insist."

"Okay, fine," she said, and that was settled. I'd seen her yesterday, I'd seen her today, and I'd see her tomorrow. I needed my daily Jude fix.

"You'll have to help me pick out a frame. I didn't even pick out the one I have now. I've never picked my own furniture. Not even when..."

There she went again, trailing off as if she'd come too close to something that caused her pain. By reading between the very obvious lines, whatever had happened had been when she didn't live here. My money was on a broken heart and I was going with that until I heard otherwise. Nothing else in the world would make someone look as haunted as a lost love of some kind.

"I'll help you. I'm not Joanna Gaines, but I can do my best to find you something you'll like." Finally, my moment had arrived.

"Yeah, I need all the help I can get. I don't even know what I like. I've never thought about it." I could kind of tell, since the house probably hadn't been touched since her parents moved.

"Does this mean I can get rid of the deer head?" I asked. That thing freaked me out. Every time I was in her living room, I knew it was judging me.

"How about this? How about you help me decorate the house and we put all that shit in the basement so my parents don't get angry that I got rid of their stuff?" That seemed like a good compromise.

"Deal," I said, sticking my hand out, which Jude shook briefly, letting go before I could register that we'd made skin-to-skin contact.

Dolly came over and dropped her ball in front of Jude, who picked it up and made a face. "Now it's wet and sandy." Still, she threw it again for Dolly, who skidded after it.

"Gross."

"Isn't your mom in real estate?" she said and it seemed like a completely random question.

"Yeah, why?"

"Couldn't you help her? With staging houses and that kind of thing?" Oh, right, we'd been talking about decorating.

"I have no idea. I've never asked. I mean, I'm not a professional or anything. I just save a lot of pictures from the internet." Everyone did that. Plus, it felt like begging. I wouldn't be one of those people running to Mommy for a job because she couldn't get one on her own. Sure, I couldn't get a job right now, but that wasn't the point.

"Still, if you have a good eye, that might be something you could do to earn extra money. You could use my parents' house as a test."

I stared at her. "Are you serious? We were just going to get you a bed and now we're doing the whole house?" She had to be out of her mind.

"Why not? All of that furniture is so uncomfortable anyway and I don't think my parents would care. They told me if I wanted to sell the house, I could." Wow, I didn't know about that.

"So why don't you?"

She lifted one shoulder and let it fall. "Where would I go?"

"Anywhere?" I said. She could go anywhere. Hop on her motorcycle and leave everything behind. It was a thrilling and terrifying thought. I was a little jealous.

"It's all the same, I guess," she said and I could tell she was, again, uncomfortable with this subject.

Dolly saved us by coming back not with her tennis ball, but with a massive piece of driftwood.

"Dolly, no one is throwing that for you," I said as she hauled it over and dropped it and looked up at us expectantly. The driftwood was at least five feet long and about as thick as my arm in some places.

Jude picked up one end and I got the other and we counted and tried to chuck the thing, but didn't get it very far.

"That was a fail," I said, wiping my hands on my pants.

"But we tried, and that's what's important," Jude said.

"That's beautiful. You should cross-stich that on a pillow or something."

Her eyes narrowed. "I can't tell if you're being sarcastic or not."

I thought about it for a second. "Neither can I."

I laughed and in a moment she joined me and I went

weak in the knees. The two of us traversed the beach twice and I could tell that Dolly was getting worn out and so was I.

"So I'll pick you up tomorrow around eleven?" I asked. That gave me enough time to have brunch with my parents and get some more job and apartment hunting done before we left.

"Sounds good."

We made our way back to our shoes, sitting down at a picnic table that was covered in old ketchup, gum, and bird poop. Jude and I were shopping for furniture, including a bed for her. That was an intimate thing to do, but I wasn't going to back out now. Getting to spend the whole day with Jude was going to be amazing, and I hoped that I didn't make a fool of myself, or do anything to make her regret agreeing to go on the excursion with me. Let's just say the first girl I really asked out was like, "ew, no, you're a weirdo," and I think that has affected me ever since.

We'd have to travel quite far to find a place that had actual furniture. It was much easier to find all of that in Boston, but there was a bonus of having to drive far, which meant more time with her. So much Jude time.

We headed back to the car with a wet and sandy Dolly. I did my best to get the sand off her feet, but I was going to have to hose her down when we got home before I let her in the house.

"This was nice," Jude said, leaning her elbow on the window, her eyes half-closed.

"I'm glad you came," I said, and then hoped that wasn't too much.

"Me too," she said through a yawn. I decided to be quiet and not talk on the way back and when we arrived in the driveway, I had to wake her up.

"Sorry," she said. "I'm not usually like this. I'm normally a night owl. Guess I'm just tired today." It was pretty late, and she'd gone out fishing today. She really needed to get her sleep under control.

"Well, go to bed," I teased.

"Yeah, yeah." She yawned again. She stumbled a little bit walking toward the house and I asked her if she needed any help, but she waved me off. "See you tomorrow."

I waited until she made it inside and shut the door before I took Dolly to the hose outside and tried to get off the worst of the sand before grabbing an extra towel from my car and drying her off as best I could.

"Come on, girl, let's go to bed." She dashed inside the house and I tried not to make much noise as I got ready for bed.

I was going to spend the whole day with Jude and I was beyond excited. My crush was growing by the hour and I was in so much trouble. I'd had other crushes before, but none like this. It had hit me suddenly and with an intensity that kept getting more...intense.

"Do you like Jude?" I asked Dolly once we got in bed.

She just looked at me with those soulful eyes and sighed.

"Yeah, I know. Stop judging me."
She closed her eyes and settled her chin in her paws.
"It's just a crush."

Chapter Eight

Jude

I had no idea why I'd agreed to let Iris take me furniture shopping and redecorate my parents' house. I was blaming it on boredom. I hadn't had much social interaction with anyone, and she was new and shiny and bright and bubbly and the attraction was hard to fight.

I couldn't let myself be attracted to her. I'd just have to find all the things that I didn't like about her and keep thinking about them to turn off that attraction. I could talk my brain out of anything if I worked hard enough at it.

I didn't want to feel anything about Iris. I didn't want to feel anything about anything.

★ ★ ★

I didn't have her number or else I might have sent a cow-ardly text to her in the morning and said I was sick and couldn't go. The downside of that, though, was that she could just march right over and see for herself. Plus, she'd probably bring me soup or something and try to be my nurse, and then I'd have to pretend to be sick. That would be more work than sucking it up and going with her.

I slept in later than I had in years. It was strange, to wake up and see the sun already in the sky. I blinked in the light and looked at my phone. It was past eight. Holy shit. I'd fallen asleep working with my new yarn, so I had to un-tangle my hands and arms from my project. I stretched on the couch and ran my hands a few times through my hair to comb it. My shoulder twinged and I hoped I didn't have to go to the doctor. It had been bothering me for a few days, but it wasn't bad enough to be alarming, just bad enough to be annoying. If I was just careful, it would heal on its own.

I got up and shuffled my way to the kitchen to get some coffee before I made some quick eggs, bacon, and toast.

I had a second cup of coffee on the porch and savored the time I had to myself. I should probably work less. I could work less. I threw myself into it because it kept me busy, but it was taking a toll on my body and my sleep.

After a leisurely shower, I still had a bunch of time before I was supposed to go shopping with Iris, so I picked up my crochet project again. I was working on granny squares, which were supposed to be really easy, but had been giv-ing me trouble. My fingers just weren't cooperating with me lately, or maybe it was that I was too distracted by a girl next door.

I had no idea what she was going to come up with in terms of redecorating. I wandered around the house, looking at all the furniture I resented and hated at this point. Growing up, I'd never thought about it; this was just my house. Now it was technically mine and I could do whatever the hell I wanted with it. I did have the feeling if I completely got rid of everything that my parents might be shocked, so I was going to store a lot of things, just in case. I had a whole basement and an attic if I needed.

One of the first things to go would be the couches and chairs in the living room, the deer head, and then my bedroom. My parents' bedroom was the biggest, and I did want to use it, but not until it was completely cleared out.

I started making a list on my phone of all the things we'd need and realized that I also wanted to paint the walls. Everything was dark and gloomy and outdated. I didn't know what I wanted, but I did know that it had to change. My life had been the exact same thing for two years and I was just tired of it. I was tired of isolating myself and refusing to talk to anyone and being so alone. Maybe it was Iris coming here that made me really see it. Maybe it was just time. Whatever the catalyst was, I needed to do something different. The house was going to be a start. Step two would be actually talking to people. The furniture was going to be a hell of a lot easier.

Before I knew it, there was a knock at the door. It was Iris, minus Dolly.

"I didn't want to leave her in the hot car and I doubt they'd let me bring her in the stores, so Mom is going to watch her furry grandchild today. So it's just us." Her cheeks went pink and I was beginning to wonder if Iris might have a little crush. That seemed impossible, but stranger things had happened. I was sure it was nothing, and mostly due to the fact that we were the only twenty-something lesbians in a thirty-mile radius. Crushes happened all the time. It was nothing.

"So I thought the best place to go would be Portland, since they have the most options," she said. "Brunswick is closer, but not as many places. Are you okay with a long trip?" Portland was an hour and a half away, so it wasn't a place you went to without a specific purpose. I hadn't been there in ages.

"Sounds good," I said. It was going to be a long time in a car and not on the back of my bike, but at least I didn't have to drive, so that was good.

"We can stop for lunch somewhere, since we'll be there around that time and then go from there. You can pick the lunch place. I'm good with anything. I'm guessing you probably don't want seafood?"

That made me laugh a little.

"I like lobster a lot," I said. "Not sick of it yet. But I think other people overcook it, so I'll stick with steak or chicken or something else. We got in the car and she backed out of the driveway.

"So, I like to listen to the radio when I drive, but I'll keep it off if it bugs you, and you can change the station anytime a song you don't like comes on. Deal?" She was so considerate.

No. I couldn't think about all the positive things about Iris. I needed to find more negatives.

We got in the car and Iris turned on the radio to the pop station on a low volume. They announced they were doing a throwback to oldies, and Iris squealed.

A pop song from the '80s came on and she started singing along. She stopped when I turned and looked at her.

"Sorry. I sing in the car too. Is that okay? I didn't drive much in Boston, so I did a lot of singing in the shower and when I was alone." She was cute.

No, she wasn't.

"Do whatever you want, I don't mind." I wanted to mind. I tried to get myself to mind, but it wasn't working. Grace sang in the car and I closed my eyes as if that could stop the flood of memories. I counted my breaths and hoped Iris didn't notice. It took longer than it should for me to put myself back in the present and not leave myself in the past.

Iris sang along to nearly every song and I was impressed with her knowledge of lyrics.

She had to stop for gas about an hour into the trip and asked me if I wanted anything from the station. I needed some more caffeine, so I asked her to grab me a black coffee. She came back with two coffees: mine and a latte for her, along with several bags of snacks and two bottles of water.

"I never go anywhere without snacks," she said as she filled the center console.

"Snacks are very important."

"So what kind of stuff do you think you want for the house?" she asked. "It would be good to have a general idea, but we can also figure out what you want when we go in the stores. You might think you want one thing and then decide on something completely different. Think about houses that you've been in or seen that you like and maybe write down some ideas."

I got out my phone and started making a list. "I think I want to paint the walls too. I was walking through today and it's so dark in there."

"I'm so glad you said that because I was hoping you'd be up for that. Paint can do a lot to change a room and no offense, but that house needs some help." She was right, it did.

We went to downtown Portland for lunch and found a small tapas restaurant tucked away on a side street that had good reviews online.

"This is so good," Iris said as she devoured little pieces of toast slathered in goat cheese and fig jam.

I was busy eating a BLT slider with the thickest cuts of bacon I'd ever had in my entire life.

"I wish I could get my parents to eat something like this," she said, "but they'd say it was fancy rich people food." She rolled her eyes.

"My parents used to be like that but then they retired and realized they had enough money and their friends took them to new places, so now they eat sushi and all kinds of things I never thought they would," I said.

"I wish that would happen with mine. I'm working

on vegetables right now. It's worse than toddlers. I have to cover everything with ranch dressing to get them to touch it."

I laughed. "That sounds like a lot of work."

"It is, but someone has to do it. I don't even want to think about what they were doing when I was gone." She shuddered.

"Does that make you think twice about leaving again?" I asked, finishing my last slider and moving on to a trio of little salads inside little fried cups. The first was arugula, lemon, parmesan, and heirloom tomato.

"No," she said quickly. "I can't parent my parents. I can only do my best while I'm here and put the fear in them for when I visit. I'm hoping to establish these habits now so they can keep them up. Not sure how that's going to go, but I can't set myself on fire to keep someone else warm."

"I love that quote. I've never heard it before. Maybe we should get that printed and put that on the wall. I like the idea of having a bunch of quotes around."

Iris lit up. "You can get custom canvases now. I think that's a great idea. You can just start sending me quotes when you find good ones that you like and I can look for them online."

Things were starting to take shape in my mind. I wanted clean, I wanted simple, and I wanted beautiful quotes around.

After lunch we walked down by the water and I watched the wind play with Iris's hair. She had it down today and it brushed her shoulders in the softest curls. I usually saw her with it up when she was at The Lobster Pot, or when she was cooking or home with her family.

I wanted to run my fingers through it.

No, I didn't.

Our first stop was a chain furniture store.

"Okay," she said. "We need to have a plan because if we just wander around, our brains are going to get overloaded real fast. So we'll start with one area, move on, and be really intentional. You tell me immediately what you like and don't like and we can take pictures. This doesn't have to be done all in one day. No pressure." She should do this as a job. She was amazing at making me feel completely at ease. Iris was so much like her mother that way: always giving of herself to others and making sure they were cared for and comfortable first. She didn't even know she was doing it, which made it all the more pure and precious.

"Sounds good," I said and we walked in. The store was four levels and completely massive. Iris steered me toward the beds first.

"So, let's start with size. What size do you want?"

I'd been sleeping on a queen and it was fine, but I wanted something bigger, even if I was the only one sleeping in it.

"King," I said.

"Great. Now, what kind of frame do you want?"

A salesperson came over and asked if we needed any help and Iris said we were just browsing and we'd come find them if we needed anything.

"I don't want them trying to sell you something you

don't want just because they need to get rid of it," Iris said under her breath. "Like, no offense, but we got this."

We walked up and down the lines of bed frames.

"Do you like this one?" she said, pointing at one that had a tufted back with gray fabric.

"I don't think so," I said.

Iris made a note on her phone, like she'd been doing since we walked in. "Then that's a no. If it's not a definite yes, then it's a no. I mean, you can always change your mind, but you seem like a decisive person."

I used to be. Life had changed that.

"That's an interesting way of looking at things. What if I don't like anything?"

"Then we go to another store," she said, moving on to the next bed that had a black leather frame and was simpler.

"No, I think it's too dark," I said, so we moved to the next, a simple wood frame that was painted white. "Now I like this." I could see sleeping in it. Classic and clean.

"Yay! We have a bed frame." Iris took a picture of it and I checked the price tag.

"That seems like a lot?" I said and Iris winced.

"Yeah, I think we could find something similar somewhere else for a better price, or even online."

Next was mattresses, and Iris made me lie on each and every bed and hopped up next to me.

"This one," I said when I'd found the right one that both supported my back and wasn't too hard.

"Oh, this is nice. I don't feel like I've ever slept on a decent mattress in my life. This is some fancy memory foam shit," she said and I turned my head to look at her and she met my eyes with a smile on her face.

"You should pick one out," I said.

"Honestly, after laying on all of them, I like this one too. But I don't think I can pull the trigger and buy a new bed yet. Need to save some more money first."

"You should do it. You need it."

She sighed.

"You don't deserve to sleep on a shitty bed," I said.

"Neither do you."

"Then I guess we're both getting beds today." I hopped off the bed and flagged down a salesperson. "Are you getting a queen?" I asked Iris.

She hesitated. "Fuck it, I'm getting a queen bed. I deserve a queen bed." Yes, she did. "I'd get a king but that definitely wouldn't fit in my room."

We both put in orders for mattresses and cringed when we saw the delivery fees, but I pulled out my card anyway.

"There goes all my tip money I guess," Iris said when she saw her total. "But I would have needed to get a new bed anyway, so this is an investment and I'll just work some extra hours to put that money back in my Boston fund. Now I just need a new frame and I'm done. I didn't see anything I really liked here. I want something a little quirkier. There's another place I want to go that I think might have something."

We moved from the beds to the couches and chairs.

"So, what kind of mood do you want to set in the living room?" she asked. "You can do different colors for different areas, or you can pick a theme for each room. I'd suggest doing an overall theme and then adding other pieces, but let's get the base down." She handed me a book of swatches to find out what colors I liked and then it was time to sit on all the couches.

"Oh, I like this," I said, sitting on one that was especially deep. I wasn't going to tell Iris that I often slept more on the couch than in my bed and needed something that would be almost as good as a mattress.

"Perfect," Iris said. "And it's on sale! Lucky us. Now what color are you thinking?"

I flipped through the swatches again and tried to picture how a whole couch would look. "I like this," I said, showing her a muted dark blue.

"Gorgeous. So with the white bed, it seems like you want to go for a coastal, nautical look? Maybe with lots of blue and white and some pops of gray or red?"

As soon as she said it out loud, I realized that was what I wanted.

"You know I was thinking," she said, getting animated and using her hands to try and paint me a picture. "You could do a bunch of buoy pictures above the couch with the motivational quotes, and sprinkle lobster stuff throughout in subtle ways. Unless you're kind of sick of lobsters."

I told her I wasn't, and she started pulling up a few items on her phone and it seemed like it was starting to come together. We had a ton of work to do.

"I'm going to pay you," I blurted out and she blinked.

"What?"

"I'm going to pay you to be my designer. People do this for a job. You be my designer and I'll pay you and you can completely redo my house." There. Then she would have more money for her bed and she wouldn't feel guilty about it.

"You're not paying me," she said. "That's ridiculous."

"No, me using you for free labor just because you're a kind person is ridiculous. You're getting paid, Iris. Don't argue."

We both knew she needed the money to get out of here. One of us should.

She stared at me and blinked a few times. "Bossy, aren't you? Okay, fine. Pay me. But it better not be a lot."

"I'll be the judge of that," I said, getting up and going to find a salesperson so I could order two couches.

Iris found her bed at the next store. The frame was completely different from mine, curving iron that looked almost antique with swirls and curves and small flowers. A bed fit for a princess.

"This is it," she said with a sigh, gazing at it in adoration.

"I'm glad you're happy."

She beamed and I told myself not to smile back at her and failed.

"I'll just have to teach Dolly not to chew it. She's a good girl but she goes wild sometimes when she's bored." Iris ordered the bed and we wandered around the store, picking out lamps and side tables and talking about paint colors.

"We can have a painting party. It's hard to get it done

all by yourself, especially with that whole house to do," she said. "I'll come over and help in my capacity as your interior designer."

She was so happy that she was glowing. I walked close to her, feeling bathed in her light. Other people noticed her too. Heads would turn as she walked by, and it wasn't just my imagination.

We decided on food again and headed to a chain restaurant/bar nearby to get chicken wings and cheap beer.

"I have a confession to make," Iris said when we were handed the massive drink menus.

"What's that?" I scanned to see what kind of beer I wanted to order.

"I kind of hate beer," she said, and I set my menu down.

"You do? Why do you keep drinking it with me?" I had no indication that she felt this way.

"Because I didn't want to be rude?" she said with a sheepish smile.

"It's not rude to tell someone you don't like something, even if they offer it to you. Jesus, Iris. Don't do things you don't want to do."

She sighed and looked at her menu. "That's easy enough to say, but not so easy to practice."

"Then you just need more practice. Do you want a beer?"

She looked at me as if I had lost my mind. I nodded at her to tell me. "No, thank you. I don't like beer."

"See? How hard was that?"

She laughed and shook her head at me.

One beer, one mojito, a bucket of wings, and a basket of fries later, I was tapped out. Chronic sleep deprivation was finally taking its toll on me.

"You ready to go, or did you want to look at some paint colors?" Iris asked.

"I'm done for today. Maybe next weekend?" I shouldn't be making so many plans with her, let alone hiring her for a project that was going to take a considerable amount of time and would require us to constantly interact.

I hadn't made so many bad decisions at once in years. It was a trend I needed to work on.

"Works for me. It's nice to get out of the house and not be tending to my parents. It wears on me after a while." She did look tired. Add up working so many hours at The Lobster Pot and trying to get her parents to eat vegetables and helping her dad and dealing with being back to a place she didn't want to be and there was a *lot*.

"You should take better care of yourself," I said, and then realized that it sounded patronizing.

"I'd say the same to you, Jude," she said, smirking at me. I didn't think she drank a whole lot because her cheeks were flushed from the one drink.

"We should motivate each other." Why did I keep saying the wrong things?

"Sounds good. You get more sleep and I'll take more time for myself."

I was making all kinds of deals and promises to her that I shouldn't be making. Yet I kept making them.

I had to stop, or else I was in real trouble.

★ ★ ★

I ate dinner alone that night and spent more time thinking about the house and what I wanted to do with it. I even started moving some things down to the basement, or up to the attic. I was going to need help for some of the bigger pieces. I didn't want to hire to get that done, but I might have to.

I scrolled through quotes on my phone and sent one to Iris. We'd finally exchanged numbers so we could talk whenever we wanted. I'd made a rule not to contact her for twenty-four hours, but then I broke it less than five hours later.

"Each morning we are born again. What we do today is what matters most."

She answered back right away.

I like that. Definitely one that should go on the wall. I'll start looking and see if there are any good prints. Oh, I also saw these and thought of you.

She forwarded some framed pictures of different lobsters done in watercolor that were a little abstract. It took me a moment, but I decided that I liked them. I asked her for the link and went ahead and bought them.

I thought that would be the end of it, but then she sent me more things and I told her whether I liked them. I bought a few more items based on her suggestions. This was really starting to come together.

We talked back and forth for hours. It was easier to talk to her this way, and open up a little more. I knew that I shouldn't, I was playing with fire, but I was so starved for any kind of connection that everything kind of spilled out at once.

Wait, you have an MBA? she asked when I told her that I'd gone to college.

Yeah, that was my parents' idea. You're not the only one who caves to parental pressure.

It was one of the biggest regrets of my life. Sure, I'd learned how to manage a business, but the whole thing had been completely soul sucking. I'd worn business casual out-fits every day and had gotten a non-gay haircut. The only thing I didn't regret about it was that I'd met Grace. She was the one bright spot in that whole nightmare.

I hadn't told Iris about Grace and I didn't want to. That was a door that needed to remain closed.

I did open other doors, talking about the places I'd lived in, which was my favorite, which state had the best pizza. Iris stumped me by asking about what I would do for a job if I could do anything, but I'd shared enough for one night, so I told her I was going to bed and ended things there.

What was I doing? I was getting too close, too fast. I needed to slow down, but I didn't know how. I spent the rest of the night trying to figure it out.

Chapter Nine

Iris

I scrolled through the text messages the next morning to make sure the conversation with Jude had actually happened and it wasn't the result of a fever dream. No, there were the texts. The messages where Jude had actually talked about herself. I almost wanted to ask if her phone had been hacked, but I just kept asking more and more questions. There were still definitely holes that I could see where she purposely wasn't talking about something. I had my theories, but I didn't want to be completely wrong, so I tried to minimize the speculation.

I couldn't believe that Jude was going to pay me to decorate her house. I had completely gone overboard with looking for things she might like and texting them to her. That was probably why she'd said she was going to bed and abruptly ended things last night. It also had been really late and I felt guilty for keeping her up.

I didn't bother her the next day, but I couldn't stop thinking about her as I spent all day at work, trying to focus on customers and orders and cleaning tables and dealing with the slackers.

"I am losing my mind," I told Anya, my only friend (other than Cindy, but she was more like a mother figure than a friend) at work.

"What's happening?" she asked as she pulled a few salads from the fridge. She added them to one of the massive red trays that was piled high with lobsters and steamers and bowls of clarified butter.

"Just...my brain." I couldn't even form words.

"Go take a break. Aren't you overdue?"

I glanced at the clock and realized she was right.

"Go," she said again and before she could change her mind, I scurried into the back and opened the rear door to sit on the steps that led downstairs. The fresh sea air was a contrast to the steamy kitchen.

I closed my eyes and inhaled deeply.

"You need to talk about anything?" I opened my eyes to find Anya looking at me. It was too bad she was extremely heterosexual, because she was one of the prettiest people I'd ever seen in my life. Her face was so perfect that I couldn't believe she was real. She'd admitted to me once that she'd done some modeling work, but hadn't liked doing it so she'd stopped. If only we were all so beautiful. She was also smart too, getting a degree in chemistry. This was only her summer work exchange gig to make money before going back to school in Germany.

"No, I'm fine," I said. "I'm just overloaded."

Anya pulled out her vape pen and took a hit. She was trying to quit smoking by switching to vaping. The vanilla-scented smoke curled in the air.

"Do you need me to make the lobsters dance?"

I laughed. "No, that's okay." In addition to doing voices for the lobsters, she also made up little dance routines and sang.

"You sure?" She turned her head to the side and blew out some more vapor.

"Is it hard for you? Being away from your family."

She shrugged. "Yes and no. I miss them, but there are so many ways to stay in touch. We video chat every day, and I'll see them soon."

I asked her how her sister, who was trying to get into college in the US, was doing, and then it was time to get back to work.

I leaned my head on her shoulder and she patted it. I said, "You saved me from a breakdown and you didn't even need to use the lobsters this time. Thank you."

"You're welcome, my American friend."

Work finally ended and I decided to bring home fish and chips for dinner for my parents so they wouldn't have to cook.

"How was work?" Mom asked and I talked about my day and asked about hers. Dad chatted about his books and then mom asked me how Jude was.

"Not sure. Haven't talked to her today."

From where I was sitting, I had a perfect view out the window of Jude's house. The lights were on and every now and then I saw a shadow move. She was over there. So close, but so far from me. I wanted to go over and see her, but I didn't want to be too much. I'd wait for her to reach out and let me know that she wanted to see me. I'd die if I annoyed her and she cut off all contact. Plus, then I wouldn't get to decorate her house and I was really excited about that. I hadn't been really excited about something in a while, which was pretty sad. Hey, at least I was getting paid. Jude and I hadn't talked about rates or anything. I hoped she wasn't going to give me too much.

"You should go over and check on her," Mom said.

"Why? She's a grown adult. She doesn't need someone to check on her," I said.

Mom just gave me a look. "Go over and blame it on me if you want. But go see her."

"Just go, baby girl," Dad said, as if I was being the unreasonable one.

"Fine, fine." Maybe they were trying to get rid of me so they could have some alone time. Gross. I didn't want to think about my parents doing...that. Or, a less gross thought, was they were trying to set me up with Jude. I hoped that was the reason.

I didn't have anything to bring her, but I think that was okay. I was definitely going to blame it on my parents.

She answered the door and there were dark circles carved under her eyes. I didn't want to tell her that she looked exhausted, but she looked exhausted.

"Hey, can I come in?" Dolly had come with me. I didn't want her in the house if my parents were going to be getting busy. Dolly didn't need to see that. It was bad enough when I had to masturbate and she sometimes made eye contact.

"Sure," Jude said, as if she was completely defeated.

"You okay? My parents sent me over to see how you were. They seem to be overly concerned about you since you came over. I have no idea."

She gave me a puzzled look, but then sighed and sort of crumpled. "Do you mind if we go sit down. I'm just…really tired. Today was rough."

I couldn't help but be concerned. "Yeah, of course, go sit on the couch. Do you want me to bring you some tea?"

She closed her eyes and sunk down on the couch. "That would be great, thank you."

I put the kettle on and found some chamomile tea. I figured I could use some calm as well and put a bag in my cup, and then added honey to both.

I brought Jude's tea. Her eyes were closed and I thought she might be asleep.

"Here you go," I said softly. "I can go if you want to go to bed. That's no problem." Unless my parents were in the middle of something, but I would go sit in my damn car if I had to.

"No, I'm fine. Thanks." She rallied and we both waited for our tea to cool enough to drink.

"Was it a rough day?" I asked.

"Yeah. I think I might have to go down to five days a week. It's just wearing on me and my shoulder has been hurting." She started rolling her shoulder back and forth and wincing. I thought about offering to give her a massage, but that would definitely be too much and she'd sense I had ulterior motives right away.

"You should book yourself a massage in town," I said instead. "You deserve it."

She made a face. "I don't know about that."

I pointed at her with the spoon I'd used to stir my tea. "Hey, remember how we agreed to be better at self-care? Getting a massage is self-care. Your body works hard and you need to take care of it. So book yourself a damn massage, Jude." Now that we'd spent more time together, it was easier to talk to her like that.

"Fine, fine. I'll let a stranger fix my body. But I'm not going to enjoy it." Jude was grumpy when she was tired and it just made me want her more. Was I attracted to grumps? I guess I was attracted to this particular grump.

"You will enjoy it. Now drink your tea."

She did and sighed. "That's good, thanks."

"Are you up for looking at more house stuff? Or would that be too much?"

She shook her head and set her tea down. "No, I can look at stuff. What have you got?"

I moved to sit next to her on the couch so I could pull things up on my phone and show them to her.

"So I was thinking we could do an anchor theme for the bathrooms, and I found this great rug," I said, grabbing the screenshot I'd taken. Jude leaned closer, almost touching my shoulder with her chin. I forgot how to breathe for a few seconds. We'd never been this close before.

She smelled just faintly of seawater and cinnamon. If I turned my head, our mouths would be close enough to touch. I kept my gaze on my phone, but my heart started racing as if it was running a marathon. I struggled to keep my voice even.

"I like that," she said and I heard her swallow. I glanced back just a tiny amount and found her gaze on my face. I stopped breathing for a second.

I smelled the honey on her breath as she replied. "I like the anchor theme."

"Me too," I said, trying to swallow and failing. My phone almost slipped from my fingers as I leaned just a fraction closer.

Then Dolly barked, and we flew apart as if a fire alarm had sounded.

"What the fuck, Dolly?" I said, trying not to scream. It wasn't her fault that we'd been having another moment. Dolly was at the window, barking like mad at something outside. I squinted into the dark and saw a black and white shape lumbering through the yard between the two houses.

"Skunk," I said, turning around to tell Jude why Dolly was freaking out, but she was right behind me.

"Oh, that's Larry. He comes around every now and then."

"Larry?" I asked.

"It seemed like a skunk name," Jude said.

"Fair enough."

"You should stay in here until it leaves. Don't want you to have to give Dolly a tomato juice bath."

Yeah, that didn't sound like fun. Dolly hadn't had as many encounters with wildlife in Boston with the exceptions of squirrels and other dogs. A skunk was something she'd probably never seen before. She looked up to me as if she was begging to go play with the new friend, but there was no way in hell.

"Sorry, Dolly Parton. That's going to be a no." She whined and wagged her tail and looked outside. "No matter how cute you are, you're not playing with Larry the Skunk. Go lay down." I snapped my fingers and she huffed and whined, but she went and lay down on the floor, glaring at me the whole time.

"Oh, she is mad," Jude said. "Look at her."

"Too bad, so sad," I said. "She'll get over it."

Jude stood only two feet away from me and there it was: another moment. Another skipped heartbeat, another held breath.

She closed her eyes and stepped away. I wanted to say something. Wanted to ask her what these moments meant to her, but she sat on the couch and picked up her tea, as if nothing had happened.

After a few moments of Jude not saying anything, I gave up and went to sit down again.

"So, anchors," she said. "I like anchors. And I think I want to do mostly white for the walls, but do one dark blue accent wall in here." Guess we were moving on and talking about the house again. I sat down with shaky legs and tried to unscramble my thoughts.

"You could do a nice statement wall right here," I said, pointing to the wall that was behind the couches and between the living room and dining room/kitchen.

"I'm not sure if it would be wise to paint before we get the furniture, or do that after."

"It would be best to clear all this out and do one room at a time, so you don't get overwhelmed." Right now I was overwhelmed. Just being in the same room with her was doing all kinds of things to me.

"You feel like helping me move all this shit to the basement?" Jude said, waving her hand around. "I would do it myself, but I can't afford to fuck up my shoulder because then I can't haul."

"Is that including the books?" One entire wall of the living room was bookshelves and they were full.

"No, I'll do those myself. I'm going to pack them up and put them in the attic. It'll just be everything else." That wasn't too bad. Two couches, a few chairs, some end tables and lamps, a coffee table.

"I know they can be kind of tacky, but what would

you think about a coffee table made out of a lobster trap? I know they're all metal now, but maybe you could find one somewhere?"

Jude stood up. "Come with me."

I looked outside. "Larry is out there."

She laughed softly at me. "We're not going outside."

She headed toward the kitchen and I followed her. She opened a door that I hadn't noticed before and turned on a light. This must be the stairs to the basement.

"Is this where you murder me?" I asked and her face got serious.

"Maybe."

My eyes went wide and she laughed. Really laughed as we walked down the stairs together. I wanted to bottle that sound and keep it forever, but that's why laughs were so precious. You couldn't keep them forever.

"Seriously, you're not going to take me into your murder basement, are you?" The stairs were carpeted and I realized as we got further down that the basement was finished. Thank goodness.

"So the guy I bought my boat from also happened to have a huge collection of wooden traps. Look to your left." I did and there was a wall of wooden traps all stacked up.

"Holy shit. That's…a lot of traps. And he sold them to you?"

Jude nodded. "Yeah, it was really sad. He'd lost his wife and was retiring and he resented his job for taking him away from his family so much. He gave me a really good deal and threw in the traps and I couldn't say no, so here they are. I've been wondering what to do with them, but I figure maybe I could try my hand at making a coffee table, and if it turns out well, maybe I could make a few more? I don't know." Dolly had given up on the skunk and had decided to follow us and investigate. She went right over to the traps and started inspecting them.

"That's a fucking amazing idea. I bet you could sell them as vintage traps. Tourists would pay through the nose for that. You could charge whatever you wanted. I could help you take pictures and set up a website. Or I could try."

Jude put her hands up.

"Whoa, let's slow down. It was just an idea."

"A damn good idea," I said.

She wanted to argue, I think, but I bet she was too tired.

"You make the first one and then we'll see." I was also going to do my own research and figure out how much she could get. "I mean, if you sold them as vintage and made by a real Maine lobsterman, look out. Those babies would sell themselves. Then you could fish less and sleep more."

"Good point." Jude yawned and stretched. "It's late."

"Yeah, I should go back over." I didn't want to. I hoped I'd given my parents enough time to do whatever they were going to do, if they were going to do something. Ew.

"Thanks for everything with the house. And the mean encouragement."

I laughed. "That's one way of putting it, but sometimes you need a little kick in the ass to feel like it's okay to take care of yourself."

"True. Okay, I'll see you later." She petted Dolly on the

head and I made sure the yard was skunk free before I let Dolly rush through the door and back over to the other house.

I listened by the front door before I walked into the house to find my parents in the living room.

No skunks, no mid-coitus parents. A successful evening.

A lot happened in the next week. My bed was delivered and they took away the twin-sized one to donate to charity, I hung out more with Jude and we ordered a ton of stuff for her house, and I went to my first meeting of the queer group at the library. I hadn't planned on it, but I was bored at home and needed to talk to someone, and I figured I could at least hang with Gladys and her wife if I didn't see anyone else that I wanted to talk to.

It was weird to be at the library at night, but I followed the sounds of laughter to a room in the back and was shocked to see about fifteen people sitting and standing and talking while they munched on snacks. I hadn't brought anything, I realized too late. Oh, well, next time.

"Iris, good to see you," Gladys said, coming over to squeeze my arm. Her hair was down on her shoulders in soft waves. Her sweater had beautiful ivory buttons and I wondered if she'd made it herself. "Come meet my wife, Mary." She led me over to a woman with dark hair that was streaked with gray.

"Oh, okay," I said belatedly.

"Mary, this is Iris. She's Kevin Turner's daughter."

"So nice to meet you." Mary had the sweetest, roundest face and I instantly relaxed when she shook my hand.

"Come meet the rest of the group," Gladys said. "I think there are some people you might know." She introduced me around, including listing everyone's pronouns. "I'm sorry, I hadn't asked yours."

"She/her," I said. I tried to remember names and pronouns, but I almost fell over when she got to someone I recognized. "Marina?"

She looked completely different, but those eyes were unmistakable.

"Yup," she said, her cheeks getting a little red. The more I looked at her, the more I saw the girl I went to school with. It hadn't been that long and the only difference was that her dark hair was at her shoulders now. In school it had been all the way down her back and she'd waltzed down the hall with it swinging like a model on a runway.

"Um, how are you?" I asked. I hated how awkward this was. Not to mention I was still holding a grudge against her for just being so insufferable for four years of my life.

"Good, good. This is my girlfriend, Jace." She waved over another girl, whose head was almost shaved except for a tiny bit on top that she'd spiked. I didn't know her.

"Oh," I said, looking from Marina to Jace. They were gay. They were gay and I was gay. "It's nice to meet you." I scrambled to get myself together after that little revelation.

"Same." Jace smiled, then looked from me to Marina and back. "I'm going to get some cheese, you want anything, babe?" There was an unasked question between the two and I watched, still shocked by the turn of events.

"No, I'm fine. Thank you." Marina gave Jace a kiss on the cheek and turned her attention back to me. "So, you're back in town. That's what I'd heard anyway. Are you staying for good?"

Great, now I had to make small talk with Marina. Why had I decided this meeting was a good idea? My eyes started drifting toward the emergency exits.

"Just temporarily. What about you?"

I had to admit, part of me was dying to know what she'd been up to since high school, because it was apparently a lot.

"Yeah, I'm here for good. I convinced Jace to come with me. I'm working for Dad."

Her parents owned a chain of discount stores with locations all over the state that had been started by her grandparents and had settled in Salty Cove decades ago. They were the richest people in town and they made sure everyone knew it.

I watched her face and she kept shuffling from one foot to the other.

"Listen, this might not be the right place, but whatever," she said. "I'm really sorry for all the shit I did in high school. I know that probably doesn't mean much, coming from me, but I was a real asshole. There's no excuse, but I was dealing with a lot. It took me two years to get the courage to come out to my parents after high school. I'm really sorry, Iris. I am."

I almost fell over and I was standing still.

"Uh, thank you. I appreciate that."

"I'm sorry about the rumors and everything. I felt awful about everything, but I think I was deflecting the attention from me to someone else. Basically, I threw you under the bus. It was a shitty, shitty thing to do. I think about it all the time."

There were tears in her eyes and I could tell she was sincere. It might take me a while to absorb this apology and process whether I wanted to forgive her or not.

"Okay, everyone, how about we get started?" Gladys clapped her hands and we all sat down.

I didn't know there would be an actual agenda, but it was really just Gladys reading news items and asking if anyone had anything they wanted to talk about, or needed support on. A few people spoke, talking about the difficulties with coming out at work, or dealing with homophobic relatives. Gladys introduced me and had everyone say their names again.

I went for the snacks and met a few more people, including several who had been at school with me either a few years before or a few years after. According to Gladys, this was a smaller meeting, since sometimes the group had swelled to almost fifty. My mouth dropped open.

I'd always thought this place hadn't had a queer community, but it had been there all along. I just hadn't known about it.

I had a lot of revelations that night and I wanted to share them all with one person: Jude.

★ ★ ★

I told her everything when I went over to her house on Saturday. She still needed some major furniture pieces, and we had to get paint.

"You want to come with me next time?" She didn't seem as excited as I thought she might be.

"I'll think about it." That was basically a no. I wanted to ask her why she was so reluctant to talk to another human, but it had to do with the big bad thing that had happened to her, as I was calling it.

We moved everything out of the living room, and the new couches and chairs and tables had arrived, and Jude had cleared out the bookcase and was slowly replacing it with her own books.

Next week we'd paint. Jude was going to take some days off for that, and I was going to help when I wasn't at The Lobster Pot. I'd taken on more hours and I was running myself ragged, but I needed a shit ton of money for going back to Boston. My plan was to get through to August and then try to get an apartment for September first. I needed a deadline, or else I wasn't going to push myself. I still wasn't getting any traction on interviews, but I knew I had to be patient.

I hadn't talked to my parents about my job-finding failures, but when I got home from work on Thursday night, the air was weird at the house.

"Hey, I'm home," I said tentatively. My parents were both in the living room and the TV was off. Dad didn't have a book in his hands.

"Sit down, Iris," Mom said. They almost never called me by my name.

"Okay," I said, starting to freak out. All sorts of scenarios flew through my head and I fought rising nausea.

"What is it?" I asked after what felt like an eternity of silence. Were they getting divorced? Had someone died? Was it cancer?

"We're worried about you, baby girl."

"Why? I'm fine." Where were they going with this?

"When are you planning on leaving?" Mom asked gently.

"I'm going to find a place for September first. And I'm going to get a job and it'll all be fine." When I said the words out loud, they sounded a little foolish.

"Do you think you can get a job and an apartment and enough money for moving costs in that time?" Mom asked. "And what happens if you lose your job? You just came back and we think it would be best if you stayed put for a little while. Just a little bit longer. Then you can make a more solid plan and you won't have to take any job that will hire you, or just any apartment. Be strategic and smart about this, Iris. You don't want to put yourself in a bad situation."

I was a grown woman, but right now I felt like a toddler. I wiped at tears and didn't know what to say. My own parents didn't believe in me and this fucking sucked.

"I'm, um, going to go for a drive," I said, getting up. "I can't do this right now."

I hated the feeling in my stomach. That I wasn't good enough. That I couldn't hack it in the big city. That what I wanted wasn't right for me. I'd made a life there that was mine. I'd gotten to decide who I was. I didn't have people assuming the person I was when I was five was still the person I was almost twenty years later. Here I was Kevin and Sarah's gay daughter. There I could just be Iris.

"Iris, wait," Mom said, but Dad held her back.

"Let her go."

I could barely walk with the tears blurring my vision, but I got in the car and managed to back out of the driveway without incident. I didn't know where I was going, only that I needed to go away for a while. If I hadn't left Dolly at home, I might have headed for Boston. I didn't know what I'd do once I got there, but that part didn't matter.

I drove and cried and sang too loud to the radio and let myself feel all the emotions and circled back to the reason that I was so upset: my parents were right. They hadn't always been, but in this instance, they were. I needed to slow down and make a better plan.

Staying here for a little bit longer would get me more money and more chances to be selective.

I drove around until I'd stopped crying and come up with another plan, what I hoped would be a better plan.

When I got back, I parked and tried to pump myself up for going back inside and admitting they were right.

I couldn't do it yet. Jude's bike was in the driveway, so I got out and knocked on her front door.

She opened it and I was treated to Jude in a tank and paint-splattered shorts. There were even little spots in her dark hair, like snow. Bonus: it was clear she wasn't wearing a bra of any kind.

Oh my. I took a few moments to try and remember why I'd come over, but I couldn't remember for the life of me.

"Hey, I was just painting. Do you want to help?" she said, holding up a roller.

"Yes," I said with a sigh of relief.

I didn't care about ruining my clothes. I could get new ones. I put my hair up using the hairband on my wrist and Jude handed me another roller. She had done one living room wall and had moved on to the second.

"I think I may have underestimated how much time it was going to take to do this. And how much my arms were going to hurt. Might have to book another massage. I went last week and you were right, damn you." Those arms were splattered with paint and her muscles were popping. I wanted to lick them, so I dipped my roller in the paint and scraped most of the excess off. I hadn't painted much, but I knew that at least.

"Oh, did you come over here for a reason? I feel like I kind of roped you into this without asking."

I started moving the roller up and down the wall. It made a slightly sticky noise as it moved that wasn't entirely unpleasant. "No, I mean…"

I wasn't sure if I wanted to tell her and then the words came spilling out anyway. I told her that my parents had sat me down and told me my plan was foolish and that after being pissed, I knew that they were right.

"I mean, it does make sense to wait until you have everything really in place," Jude said. "Even six months might make a huge difference. You can find a really good job that you love."

Exactly.

We kept painting and Jude told me about her week. It was a relief to paint and talk with her. How could I be both so relaxed and so nervous around her? I kept watching her from the corner of my eye, admiring how her muscles worked as she painted. We had to switch places a few times so I could get the bottom part of the wall and she could get the top with a longer roller. A little bit of paint dripped down and got in my hair.

"Sorry," she said, looking down at me with a grin.

Fuck, she was beautiful. Even at this angle.

"It's okay," I choked out.

We finished the wall and stood back to admire it.

"I think we need another coat," I said. I could still see a little bit of the underlying awful green. What had her parents been thinking?

"Definitely. Or two." She leaned on her roller and sighed. "At least this is keeping me busy and not thinking about things I don't want to be thinking about."

"What kind of things?" I asked, hoping she would cave and tell me.

"Nothing. No things," she said. Still not going to crack.

"Fine, fine." I set my roller down and looked at my hands. I was splattered everywhere with paint.

"Do I have more paint on me than you?" I asked her.

"I can't tell, but you're pretty well covered," she said with a laugh, coming over to wipe at something on my cheek with her thumb. The significance of the gesture was not lost on me. Her touch was gentle, yet her thumb was rough and calloused. She pulled her hand back, and for the first time, I saw Jude blush. That was another thing I wanted to bottle and save.

"Sorry," she said, but I wasn't sure what she was apologizing for.

"It's okay," I said. Then we both jumped as my phone dinged with a text message. I wiped my hands and grabbed it from where I'd set it on a table so it wouldn't get covered in paint.

It was a message from my parents asking when I was going to be back and hoping that I wasn't still upset.

I typed out a quick response that I was just helping Jude paint and I would be back in a few minutes.

"I should go. I need to go tell my parents they were right." I rolled my eyes. "Not super looking forward to that." Jude gave me a sympathetic look.

"You can always come back over here and paint with me because if I do it myself, it's going to take about a thousand years."

"I'll be back tomorrow. Don't work too much," I said, backing out of the room and then pausing for a moment at the door and looking into the yard.

"What are you doing?" she asked, coming up behind me.

"I'm looking for Larry."

"I think you're safe," Jude said in my ear and I wasn't

going to turn around. I wasn't because if I did her mouth was going to be right there and then I would want to kiss it. I couldn't deal with the temptation. So I reached for the doorknob and let myself out without looking back.

Chapter Ten

Jude

I'd started work on my first lobster trap coffee table after getting some ideas online. It was a nice break from painting, which got monotonous and I got headaches from the fumes after too long. Having Iris around to help was great and broke up the monotony. I still had barely done one room and had the rest of the house to go.

Cutting back on lobstering was, so far, going well. I did miss being out on the water so much. I was beginning to think that the time when I spent every single day out there alone was over. Things were changing. I could feel myself smiling more, laughing more. My throat actually got sore from all the talking, as if it was rusty from disuse. It reminded me of when I met Grace, after I'd wrapped myself in a bubble at school, but when I met her, I'd actually lost my voice because we talked so much in those first few days.

Since I had less time on the water, there was more time for other things, like crocheting and getting massages and thinking about my past. I was letting myself have little sips of it, here and there. Letting myself remember her laugh and her smile and the way she'd looked at me. So much had already started to fade from my mind. For the first time in probably a year, I pulled up the pictures I'd saved on my phone. I listened to her last voicemail, asking me to remember to pick up eggs, apples, and conditioner. The most mundane message, but I cherished it. I let myself hear her voice. It was both a relief and agony at the same time. I set my phone aside and went back to the basement to work on the coffee table.

I sanded the trap down and replaced the nets and painted it a soft white color and then distressed it a little. I was pretty sure I could get a few hundred dollars for it, so if I could sell just five a month, that wouldn't be too bad. I'd also started sourcing other traps, but that was harder. It was something I was going to have to work on, but so far I liked doing it.

I couldn't help feeling a little satisfied that she was sticking in Salty Cove. I'd been unconsciously counting the days until she left. Now I didn't have to think about it as much.

In a tiny corner of my mind, I thought about what if she didn't leave. What if she stayed? I didn't think she would, but every now and then, the thoughts of "what if" would get me in little moments.

No, I wasn't going to go down that particular mental path. I was going to think about other things and let that one thought slide.

It took us two more days to finish the living room, including the accent wall. We'd gone with a deep cobalt blue that was brighter than I might have chosen, but which looked incredible once it was done. I'd been worried it would clash with the blue couch, but it didn't.

"Holy shit," I said when we'd arranged everything. My lobster trap coffee table was in place, as were a few side tables, some clear glass lamps, and a few quotes for the wall, along with the abstract lobster paintings. I'd picked "Try to be a rainbow in someone's cloud" by Maya Angelou, "I dwell in possibility" from Emily Dickinson, and "Keep your face always toward the sunshine—and shadows will fall behind you" from Walt Whitman, and several others.

"I know," Iris said, looking around. "I'm really fucking good, aren't I?" Our eyes met and we both laughed.

"Yeah, you are. I'm paying you more money."

"I probably deserve it," she said, and I bumped her with my shoulder.

"Yeah, you do."

"We should celebrate," she said. "Do you have any champagne or anything?"

"I think I could find something," I said, going to the kitchen. It was after dinner and Dolly was snoozing on the new couch. Iris had tried to get her to not sit on the new couch, but I said it was fine.

I found some old champagne in the back of the fridge that my parents must have bought for New Year's.

"Will this work?" I said, holding it up.

"Only if you have cheese and crackers to go with it."

I found some of those as well and made a little snack plate before pouring us both a glass of bubbly.

"To your decorating talent," I said, raising my glass.

"To your letting me use it," she said and we touched our glasses together and then drank. It was dry and fizzy and tickled as it went down.

"Holy shit," she said, sitting up abruptly and almost spilling her entire glass.

"What?" I wondered if she'd spotted Larry, so I immediately looked out the window.

"What if I got my real estate license? I mean, I never really thought liking decorating was a real thing, but now that I've done your house, I think I might be good at it? Maybe. I'm just spitballing. I've been banging my head against a wall trying to get marketing jobs. Maybe I should change my approach. At least if I had a license that would be something extra on my résumé. Holy shit, why didn't that occur to me before?"

"That sounds like an amazing plan." It really did. I was proud of her, but I didn't want to say that. It would sound too much like I liked her.

"It doesn't sound ridiculous, does it?"

I shook my head and then sipped my champagne. "It doesn't sound ridiculous at all."

We took our crackers back into the living room to bask in how beautiful it was.

"This looks like a home of someone rich or successful or both," I said. It didn't feel like mine yet, even though I had picked everything out with Iris's help. It would take some getting used to, but I was okay with that.

"I got you something," Iris said.

"You didn't have to do that. You literally did all this." I waved my arm around.

"It's not big. It's just something small. Wait for a second." She dashed out to the porch and brought something back that was wrapped in lobster wrapping paper.

"Cute," I said.

"Thank you."

I opened it up to find a portrait of a lobster buoy that was painted exactly like mine that she'd seen stacked up in the yard in a frame that felt like driftwood. It was simple, but perfect.

"Do you like it?" she asked, and I could tell she really wanted me to like it.

"It's perfect," I said. "And I know right where it's going to go." I set it on a side table, right next to a lamp. It fit right in.

"I hoped you'd like it." I could feel her nervous energy.

I wanted to soothe her fears. "I love it." We sat next to each other on the couch and Dolly dominated the other one, as was her right. "I really love it."

I touched her shoulder. It was dangerous, allowing myself to have these little touches, but they didn't mean anything. They didn't have to mean anything.

"I'm glad," she said.

There it was, one of those moments again. We'd had so many I had lost count. I hoped they would stop affecting me, but so far, no good. Being near Iris was a constant battle of not giving in to what I wanted. What I didn't want to want.

She was so sweet and so beautiful and so kind and so wonderful. She looked nothing like Grace. No, they were as different visually as night and day. Grace also hadn't been so bubbly, or so outspoken. No, she'd been quiet like me, but we'd balanced each other out, her being more sensible and controlled, and me being the wild one with the bad ideas that got me into trouble. Grace bailed me out of more than one situation, including an almost bar fight. Her cool head was the only thing that could make me see sense. She was also a total goof and never gave up an opportunity to wear a ridiculous costume, including the time I came home and she was dressed in one of those dinosaur suits and cooking dinner like everything was completely normal. I got to see the side of Grace that no one else did. Iris was pretty much the same with everyone. Always shining bright. It was a different feeling, this thing for Iris. My feelings for Grace had been slow in coming, but once they had, they were deep and unfathomable.

It felt unfair, comparing the two of them. Grace wasn't here anymore, and Iris was.

Iris was everything bright and good in the world and I was addicted to being near her. I didn't know what I was going to do when this house project was over. I'd have to invent other ways to get her to come over on the pretense of helping me with something. I should probably help her. I could quiz her on real estate facts. I didn't even care, as long as I got to be close to her.

She leaned again and for a fraction of a second, I considered leaning too. And then I remembered why I wasn't leaning with anyone and sat back, hastily grabbing for my glass of champagne and almost knocking it over.

"What does it take to get a real estate license?" I asked, to revive the conversation.

"You really just have to pass the test, but I'm going to have to study a lot before that happens. There are classes, which I need to sign up for because I don't think I can just study and pass on my own. It's like being back in high school where I have to juggle work and school." She made a face, but I could tell she was excited.

"I can help you study. Quiz you with flash cards, whatever you need." I should reel it in before I said too much.

"Really? You'd do that? It's probably going to be really boring."

"Sure."

We were both startled as Dolly started barking her head off, going right for the window and putting her paws up on a table.

"Another Larry sighting?" I asked as Iris went to calm Dolly down.

"Yup. He's just cruising through the yard. He'd be cute if I wasn't so worried about his stinky butt." I laughed and Iris made Dolly lie back down on the couch.

I finished my first glass of champagne and poured myself another. Iris drained her glass and held it out for more.

"If I have to wait for Larry to leave, I might as well enjoy myself," she said. The champagne was going to my head, and I would have to be careful or it would let down the walls that I'd so carefully constructed to protect myself against Iris, or anyone else, getting in.

I wanted to let go. I wanted to have something I wanted. So I downed my second glass of champagne and faced her.

"What room should we do next?"

"Maybe your bedroom?" I'd officially moved into my parents' bedroom, but I'd stripped it and only had a bed. It was the only room in the house that Iris hadn't been in yet.

"Okay, we'll do that one next," I said, and finished my second glass.

Iris watched me fill up a third and she was so busy drinking she ended up losing her grip on the glass and it spilled all over the couch and fell to the floor, shattering.

"Oh, shit, I'm sorry," she said, trying to brush the liquid off the couch. I grabbed her hand to stop her.

"It's okay," I said. "Don't worry about it. We've christened the couch. Don't they always do that to boats? Smash a bottle of champagne?" She started to laugh and then looked down at my hand holding her wrist.

There was broken glass on the floor, but it didn't matter.

This time I was the one who leaned. Well, I stopped

myself from *not* leaning into her. It was much easier to let myself finally give in to what I'd been wanting since she showed up on my porch with Dolly.

Iris inhaled with surprise, and what finally broke me was the tiniest little smile that bloomed across her lips. I couldn't resist anymore.

She leaned the rest of the distance and our lips met. Hers were soft and warm and tasted of the champagne. Once I started, I couldn't help myself. I grabbed her face and drank her in. It had been so long since I'd kissed someone. So long.

I couldn't tell if it was because it had been so long, or if it was because of Iris, but it was like a spark had ignited in my chest and I'd burst into flame. She made a sound and I pulled back.

"No, I'm fine, get back here," she said and pulled my face to hers again.

This time she was the aggressive one, yanking me closer, kissing me so hard that it felt like she was trying to devour me. I let her, and I wanted to devour her back. It was a battle of lips and tongues and teeth, both of us gasping and trying to figure out the best way to kiss and breathe at the same time and failing most of the time. She practically crawled into my lap and I was moments away from making some extremely bad decisions.

I wanted to make them.

I didn't want to deal with the consequences.

My hands were full of her and she was so sweet and so warm and it had been so long since...

I pulled away.

"I'm sorry," I said to her lips that were a deeper pink from the kiss. Iris blinked at me a few times.

"Do you like me?"

I closed my eyes. I couldn't. I couldn't do this with her. A sick feeling rolled through my stomach and I needed to get away. Away from Iris, away from what we'd just done.

"I wish I didn't," I said, opening my eyes.

She looked at me with naked hurt and betrayal in her eyes.

"Why don't you want to?"

My heart pounded in my chest and I had to turn my face away from her. "I'm so sorry, Iris. I really am."

"Yeah, sure, fine."

She got off my lap and called to Dolly. She was gone and I was left with broken glass on the floor and a couch sticky with champagne.

Chapter Eleven

Iris

Seriously, what the fuck? Why couldn't she just let me in? She was willing to kiss me, but not to trust me or talk to me, and I couldn't deal with that. I stormed back to my parents' house and they both started to ask me what was wrong, but I glared and they both shut up. I headed first for an angry shower and then to my room.

I thought about transcribing all my angry thoughts into text messages, but that was mostly the champagne talking. Rationality prevailed and I angrily browsed the internet on my phone instead.

Dolly seemed to realize that I needed some comfort and put her head in my lap and nosed my phone out of the way.

"I'm okay," I said, even though I really wasn't. I didn't want Dolly to worry about me. She was such a good girl when she wasn't barking her brains out at Larry the Skunk.

Dolly whined as if she didn't believe me.

"I know, I know." I set my phone down and started petting her head. That was much more soothing than the internet any day.

There was a knock at my door.

"Yeah?" I said.

My mom cracked the door open and peeked her head in.

"Are you okay? You looked pretty upset when you came in." That was probably an understatement. I was hurt and pissed and all the other negative emotions you can have at once.

"I'm fine," I said, trying to keep my voice light.

"We both know that's not true, baby girl," she said, coming in and sitting on the edge of my bed.

"Fine, whatever." I didn't want to talk about it.

"I'm going to take a wild guess and say that something happened with Jude?"

I looked at Dolly who stared back at me. "I don't want to talk about it."

Mom knew me so she just waited. She knew that eventually I'd get tired of the silence and cave.

It took less than two minutes.

"I don't know if Jude likes me or not, and she's so closed off and I just want her to open up, but she won't. I wish I could give up on it, but I can't. She's just so fucking frustrating."

"Why do you think she doesn't want to open up?" my mom asked gently.

"There's some sort of big bad thing in her past that she always walks around like it's a live bomb. I mean, reading between the lines, it's some kind of heartbreak, but I don't know for sure because she won't tell me. And I can't force her, so I'm wondering how much more effort I should put in for someone who isn't giving it back, you know? Why do I always pick the wrong people?"

I sighed and I would never admit it, but I did feel better to talk to someone about this at last. I was looking forward to the queer group meeting next week as a distraction. Maybe Gladys would know what to do.

"Is she worth the effort, even if she doesn't open up?" Mom asked.

I had to think about that for a moment and I didn't like the answer.

"Yes. Yes she is. She's worth it. Even if she never tells me anything. At least I won't have any regrets when I leave."

Mom held her arms out and I let myself enjoy a mom hug. There really was nothing like it. If only mom hugs could make Jude tell me about her past.

"Do you want some cake or something?" she asked and I thought about saying no, but I didn't.

"Milk and cookies?" I hadn't had that in ages. She went to the kitchen and came back with a plate and two tall glasses of milk.

Mom broke her cookie in half, dipped one piece in the milk, and took a few bites. "Oh, that is good. You should bring some of these over to Jude tomorrow after she's cooled off and maybe thought things over."

I shook my head. "No way. I'm making her do the leg-work this time. If she wants to make up, she knows where to find me."

"Fair enough."

We ate the entire plate of cookies and drank all the milk. It was exactly what I needed, but when she was gone, I was left with my thoughts, which wasn't the most fun.

Jude had kissed me. She had wanted to kiss me and she did and I kissed her back and then... Then she had shut me down.

I wasn't mad that she'd stopped kissing me. Well, I was a little miffed. It had been a fucking great kiss. Probably the greatest kiss I'd ever had in my life. I wanted to kiss her again and find out if it was a fluke or not.

No, what hurt was that she'd emotionally shut me out. I understood it was hard for her to open up, but she wouldn't even try. I just wanted her to trust me. I needed her to trust me.

The ball was in her court this time. I was going to wait until she decided she wanted to talk to me. I couldn't keep throwing myself at her.

So, I would wait.

I was just preparing for the lunch rush when one of the slacker girls came and found me.

"There's someone here to see you," she said.

"Who?" I asked. I had a feeling I might know who it was, but I was probably wrong.

"I don't know. She's wearing a leather jacket."

My heart jumped into my throat. It hadn't even been a full day.

I went out to the front of the restaurant and there she was, freshly showered with her damp hair swept back from her forehead, looking like a lesbian James Dean, ready to sweep me off my feet and onto her motorcycle.

"Hey," she said, her mouth tense. "Can we talk?" She had her hands jammed into her pockets.

"Yeah, sure," I said, wiping my hands on my apron and hoping there wasn't flour or anything else on my face.

We went outside onto the deck. No one was out here yet, so we had a little bit of privacy. Jude sat down at one of the picnic tables and I sat on the other side.

"I'm sorry," she said. "I wanted to say that first. That I'm sorry that I can't open up to you. I'm sorry that I kissed you and then everything kind of got messed up. I've wanted to kiss you, Iris. I've wanted to kiss you ever since you set foot on my porch that first night." This was everything I wanted to hear, but I was waiting for the "but" to come.

"But I shouldn't have kissed you. You deserve someone who can be with you completely. You deserve everything good in the world, Iris. You deserve the best, and I'm just broken." Her words made me want to cry.

"Fuck, you're not broken, Jude," I said, reaching for her. She sighed and her jaw tensed, but she let me put my hand on hers.

"You don't know, Iris. You just don't know. Listen, I have to go now, but can I pick you up tonight?"

I was confused. "Pick me up? Like, on your bike?" My voice squeaked a little.

"Yeah, are you scared?" The teasing was back and that was a relief. I didn't know what was supposed to happen if I got on Jude's bike, but I was willing to put my terror aside and find out.

"I don't know, Jude. I just... I can't do this back and forth. It's not right."

"I know. You're right. Let me pick you up tonight and we'll talk about everything, okay?" Her chin trembled and I wondered if she was going to take it back.

"Everything?"

"Yes. I promise."

"Okay, I'll be here." Our eyes met for only a moment before she was gone again, and I was gripping onto the railing and wondering what the hell was going to happen.

I was exhausted and nervous as hell that night when I walked out to the parking lot and found Jude waiting for me. I'd skipped out a little bit early to shower and change my clothes. I'd shoved my work clothes in my backpack and hoped my hair didn't still smell of French fries. Or, if it did, that Jude was turned on by French fry smell.

"Hey," I said as she sat on the bike like some sort of fantasy come to life. My fantasy.

"Hey. You ready?" She held the helmet out to me.

"I've never been on a bike before," I said.

"Don't worry. I've got you."

I climbed on behind her and she showed me how to put my hands around her waist to hold on for dear life. I tucked my head against her back and breathed in the smell of her hair. And then we were moving and I was trying not to scream.

"It's okay," Jude yelled. "I've got you."

I realized a few minutes later that I had no idea where we were going. I guess I'd assumed that she was going to take me back to her place, but she didn't. She took me to the beach.

Jude hid the bike on the side of the road, along with the helmets.

"Come on," she said.

"You're not going to murder me on the beach, are you? Jessica Fletcher would totally catch you." She gave me a puzzled look. "Never mind."

I was going to have to get Jude to watch *Murder, She Wrote* if things changed between us and she decided she wanted some kind of relationship.

I followed her down to the sand, where we took off our shoes and started to walk. I waited for her to talk.

"I can't have a relationship, Iris. I can't. I can't do it. This thing with you…it scares me. The way I feel about you scares me." I tripped and nearly fell, but Jude caught my arm and stopped me from eating sand.

These weren't exactly the words I wanted to hear, but I think they were the words I expected.

"And?" I asked.

"And you needed to know. And I don't know where we go from here."

We kept walking, both of us lost in our thoughts. I had an idea. Probably the worst idea, but right now, I didn't care.

"We don't need to have a relationship. I mean, we could just…hang out and do other things. It won't be a relationship. It'll just be us being together while I'm here. I don't want a relationship either. It wouldn't make sense for anything long term, since I'm leaving eventually." I was lying through my teeth about what I wanted and I hoped she bought it.

Jude stopped walking. "Are you sure? You're not leaving in a few weeks, Iris. That seems like a lot. I don't want you to get hurt. My heart is already broken, but yours isn't."

"Yeah, I'm sure. We can totally have a physical-only relationship. People have done it before. We don't have to get feelings all involved. It'll be a summer fling." I couldn't believe the complete bullshit I was able to spin, but I think it was working.

"I don't want you to get hurt."

Right now I was feeling reckless from the motorcycle ride and didn't care. I also wanted her so much I could barely stand. Plus, I'd had casual sex. I could do it again.

"You know, I've had my heart broken before. I've been with other people. I'm not as fragile as you think I am. Trust me to know myself."

She gave me a long look, as if she was searching for something.

"You need to tell me if you change your mind at any point. I'm not saying yes, but I'm saying we can go back to my place and see how things go."

It was close enough.

Jude took a step closer to me and tucked some of my still-damp hair behind my ears. It was a disaster from being under the helmet.

"This is a bad idea."

"Sometimes bad ideas are the best ones," I countered and she sighed. I didn't know what my parents would think about me staying over at Jude's, but I didn't care right now. I'd send them a text. They should be thrilled if they'd been trying to set us up.

"Okay," she said. "Let's go."

Bad idea, bad idea, bad idea.

The ride to Jude's was somehow more harrowing, even though I'd kind of gotten used to the weave of the bike on the road. I stepped off with shaky legs and followed her as she walked up the steps and onto the porch.

"One last time, are you sure about this?" she asked, opening the door. We never locked our doors around here.

"Yes," I said, and pushed her through the doorway. I grabbed at her leather jacket and she made a little sound of surprise before capturing my mouth. It had been so long since I'd been close to someone like this and I was starving for it. Starving for her skin and her touch and her kiss. At my last count, it had been seven months since I'd had sex. Honestly, the last time didn't even count. It had been a hookup with a friend of a friend and it had turned awkward and weird halfway through and I still shuddered when I thought about it. That night had been a fail. I was determined that tonight wouldn't be with Jude. My last encounter had been just about sex. This thing with Jude was so much more, but I couldn't let her figure that out or she was going to put on the brakes.

"We're supposed to be talking," Jude said, breaking the kiss.

"Talking is overrated. This is just sex, Jude. We're both adults, we can handle it."

I pressed my mouth to hers again, this time using my tongue, and I felt the moment that she surrendered.

We stumbled backward while trying to kiss and remove our clothes and walk at the same time. After crashing into the couch, we both laughed.

"Let's do one thing at a time," she suggested. I didn't want to do one thing. I wanted to do them all. Logistically, I knew this wasn't possible, but I wished it was.

I settled for getting her naked. If I could have shredded her clothes with sheer will, I would have.

"Slow down," she said with a laugh as I clawed at her jacket and her shirt and her jeans, not sure which should go first.

"You do bottom, I'll do top," I said, and laughed. I didn't even care if I had made an unintentional joke. I wanted Jude naked, *now*.

I managed to get her jacket down her arms and started pulling up her shirt.

"Why do I have to lose my clothes first?" she asked, her voice muffled as I shoved her shirt over her head. She wasn't wearing a bra underneath.

"Because you're the hotter one. The hotter one always has to get naked first," I said.

"That's complete bullshit because you're definitely the hotter one in this scenario."

Now I was subject to a clothing assault and before I knew what was happening I was standing there in my bra and panties. Thank goodness I'd worn a cute pair today. I might have picked a sexier pair had I known that I would be seeing Jude without my clothes on, but I couldn't go back and I wasn't going to worry about it. I didn't think the underwear was what she wanted to see.

"You're so beautiful, Iris. Fuck."

She stroked her hands down my sides, squeezing and caressing here and there. I tried not to think about my flaws and insecurities. Being horny as hell helped.

"Come on," she said, taking my hand and leading me into her bedroom. It was bare, with the exception of her giant bed. She'd gotten dark blue sheets with a white comforter with blue piping.

"This is the second time we've been in bed together," I said and she gave me a puzzled look. "We tried beds at the mattress store."

Then I got so distracted by her breasts that I forgot what we were talking about. They were just the perfect size to cup in my hands and I went for it. She still had her jeans on, but we'd work on that. Right now I wanted to worship her top half. I was going to make the most of it in case this blew up in my face (it would), and I never got to be intimate like this with Jude again.

"You're perfect," I said, stroking her nipples with my thumbs. She let out a little gasp and arched into me.

"Fuck, it's been so long."

I didn't ask any follow-up questions. That's not what this was about. This was about two people needing a physical connection and letting themselves have it for a while.

"Same," I said, and pushed her back so she fell on the bed. I'd never been much of an aggressor in this area, but I was feeling like one tonight. I blamed the pent-up lust.

Jude put her hand on my chest to stop me from leaning down and licking her neck.

"What?" I said, my blood going cold. Was she going to stop me and say that this was a terrible idea?

"We don't have to rush," she said. "We have time."

Not enough.

"Then I'm going to take my time with you, Jude," I said. My sweet fucking time.

She moved back on the bed so I could straddle her and I thought my head was going to explode just from that. I ran my fingers through her hair, brushing it back from her face. That simple contact was at once so electric and so intimate that I didn't know how I was going to get through this without losing my heart in the process.

This wasn't the time to think with my heart. This was the time to think with my vagina.

"You're so hot, Jude," I said. I wanted her to know how

sexy she was. I had the feeling she had no idea. "Do you know how long and how often I've thought of these arms?" I stroked said arms and nearly passed out. Her muscles were warm and soft and hard at the same time.

"No?" she said.

"It's a lot. A lot a lot."

She lifted her chin in challenge.

"Show me."

I would.

I kissed her mouth until I was dizzy and then kissed my way across her cheeks and to her neck, pausing at one particular spot that made her moan, before I headed for her collarbone and across her shoulders.

I licked her biceps and nibbled at her forearms and even tried to get her triceps but she giggled and I realized she was ticklish. I stored that information away for future torture.

"Why is you biting my arms such a turn-on?" Jude moaned, her eyes fluttering open and closed.

"I don't know, but I'm glad you like it." I could spend all night here, but there were other parts of her to explore. I could always come back to the arms later.

For now it was time to worship her breasts. They were on the smaller side, but completely perfect for her. I had to fight with mine sometimes and couldn't go without a bra. I was actually a little jealous of hers.

"Sorry they're small," she said and I gave her a look.

"They're perfect, Jude. Perfect." Now I had to show her. I stroked and caressed and pinched her nipples and then leaned down and sucked one nipple into my mouth. She arched off the bed and let out a moan. Oh, she liked that. I made another note. I wanted to learn everything she liked.

I paid excruciating attention to her breasts, teasing her nipples into hard peaks, blowing on them, biting them.

"I can't take it," Jude gasped, thrashing on the bed. She still had her jeans on and I needed to do something about that. So while one hand was playing with her left nipple, the other went to work on her zipper. I wasn't super skilled at undoing someone else's zipper with one hand, so I had to abandon the nipple teasing.

"Can I take your pants off?" I asked and her eyes opened. They were glazed and her entire face was flushed.

"Uh-huh," she said and I started to pull her pants and her underwear off, but I needed her help.

"Come on, Jude." She lifted her hips so I could get her naked. I tossed the pants and undies to the other side of the room.

There she was. Completely naked. Jude was naked and I got to look at her.

I had to sit back for a moment and thank my lucky stars that I had agreed to get on her motorcycle tonight.

"I don't even know what to say," I said.

"You don't have to say anything." She stared back at me, as if she was daring me.

"What do you want?" I asked.

"What do *you* want?"

"You. I just want you," I said. It was that simple.

"I want you too," she said. "Come here." She pulled me down for a searing kiss and while I was distracted by her wicked tongue, she undid the back of my bra and then slipped the straps down my arms.

"So sneaky," I said, and she laughed. I pulled my arms out of the straps and then flung the bra to land with her jeans. Just one more scrap of fabric stood between me and complete nudity with Jude.

"I try," she said, and then her clever fingers were inching my panties down my hips. I had to do a little maneuver to get them off, but once they were, I wished I'd known we were going to do this so I could have, uh, groomed myself a little more. Not that I had a full situation going on, but I hadn't trimmed everything up in a while.

I glanced up to apologize to Jude, but she was staring at me as if I was the most beautiful thing she'd ever seen. There was a sense of awe in the way she gazed at my body. It scared me a little.

"You're incredible, Iris. Fuck, look at you."

I glanced down and didn't see much to inspire that kind of compliment. I had more fat on my body than she did, and a few more stretch marks, and definitely less muscle.

"You like?" I asked. My self-esteem wasn't bad, but it was another thing altogether to be completely vulnerable with another person like this.

"Very much. Can I show you?" I guess it was my turn to be ravished. I was ready for it. Jude and I traded places, with me lying back on the bed. Jude stared down at me and smiled. "What do you want?"

"Surprise me," I said.

That made her laugh. "I'll ask before I do anything too outrageous."

I raised one eyebrow. "Can you tell me about these outrageous things?"

"Mmm, you'll have to wait and see." She dragged one finger from my chin down my neck and between my breasts. Fuck. She was going to destroy me. "I don't think you understand all the things I've thought about. All the nights I couldn't sleep when I thought about you."

I'd done the same damn thing. I'd masturbated more in the past few weeks than I had when I was a horny high school freshman just discovering I liked girls.

"Show me," I demanded. "Show me everything."

She did.

Jude kissed my mouth until I had stopped breathing and tasted and sucked my neck, definitely leaving marks before moving to my breasts and lavishing them with attention and care. I didn't need to tell her that I liked a little bit of pain where that area was concerned. She figured that out all on her own.

"Fuck, yes, more," I moaned as she bit down on one and pinched the other with her devious fingers.

"I thought you would like that," she said, raising her head and giving me the most devilish smile as her hair fell across one eye. She slinked down my body, stopping to kiss my belly and nibble at my sides and lick my stretch marks.

"What else do you think I'd like?"

She stroked me between my legs with one hand. "I think you're going to like this."

"Yes." The word hissed from my lips as I closed my eyes and pushed myself into her hand for more contact.

"More?" she asked.

"Yes." It was the only word I currently knew how to say right now.

She stroked me again, tantalizingly slowly. Then the contact went away and I sat up, making a whimpering noise.

"Calm down, I'll get back there," Jude said with another wicked smile. "I'm going to take my time with you, Iris." I made an involuntary sound of frustration and Jude laughed. "Just wait." She dragged one finger up the inside of my right thigh. "I have to give your legs some attention first. They're incredible and attention must be paid."

I tried to argue, but then she grabbed one of my feet and kissed the bottom of it and I had no idea that would feel so good, but it did. Jude proceeded to kiss my feet, then my calves, then my shins, my knees, the tops of my thighs.

She paid excruciating attention to my legs and it was maddening and arousing all at once. Most of my other sexual encounters had been awkward and fumbling and I had never really felt like I was doing the right thing, or that the other person was having a good time, or was really into me.

I wasn't worried about Jude. She treated my body with reverence and complete decadence, as if I was the most delicious thing she'd ever held or tasted or experienced.

She wasn't hesitant or unsure of herself. The moment she took charge, she put me at her mercy.

I loved every second of it.

Jude pushed my legs apart and scooted down until she was right between them, pausing just long enough to make eye contact with me that left no doubt in my mind what she was about to do.

She waited for a heartbeat to give me the chance to stop her, but I didn't want her to stop. I wanted her to completely destroy me, heart and all.

"Oh, fuck," I said at the first touch of her tongue. She started slow, tasting, teasing. Gentle little licks that were completely earth shattering and made me writhe on the bed and beg for more.

Then she added her fingers and I was lost. I came so hard and so fast that I'm pretty sure I blacked out for a few seconds as the bursts of pleasure overtook me, burning through me like fire.

Jude popped her head up and wiped her face, and there was a catbird grin on her face. Someone was pleased with themselves.

"That was fast," she said.

"Is that a compliment? I can't tell." My body was warm and loose. I could have just closed my eyes and gone right to sleep. But I wouldn't. It was her turn to be ravished.

"I'm not sure," she said. "It's been a little while since I did this and I'm trying to remember how it works."

I pushed her hair back from her face. "You shouldn't have said anything because I was under the impression you were completely in control and knew exactly what you were doing."

She shrugged and flopped on her back beside me.

"Hey," I said, propping myself up on my elbows and looking at her.

"Hey," she said.

"Let's switch places. It's your turn."

She waved me off. "You don't have to do that. Tonight is all about you. Just let me know when you're ready again."

Was she out of her mind?

"Um, hell no. You're not going to deprive me of making you come. Rude." I sat up and slid down the bed, nearly falling off in my attempt to get on top of her.

"No, really, you don't have to. It's late and—" I shut her up with a kiss.

"Stop it," I said. "Unless you don't want to, which is totally fine. But I want to make you come. I haven't been able to stop thinking about it. You're not a burden, Jude. I don't know who made you feel like that, but I want to punch them."

"You don't have to punch anyone, Iris. There isn't any-one *to* punch."

I stroked the side of her face and she leaned into my hand.

"But if you needed me to, I would," I said and kissed her again.

Chapter Twelve

Jude

I liked the way she looked at me. I liked the way she smiled at me. I liked the way she touched me, as if I was something precious.

Iris kissed me hard and deep and our tongues tangled together as she stroked her hand up and down my belly, moving it ever closer to where I needed her most. I lifted my hips to urge her to move a little faster, but she just laughed.

"Who's the impatient one now?" she said, her blue eyes sparkling with mischief.

Seeing her like this was amazing. Not as amazing as watching her come apart under my hands and tongue. I was still completely drunk on the power of making her or-

gasm. I wanted to do it again and again, which was why
I'd stopped myself. If I wasn't careful, I would let myself
completely give in and make her come until she literally
couldn't take it any more. And then I'd make her breakfast and serve her in bed and wait until she got her strength
back and fuck her again and again.

I could fall for Iris. I could fall so, so easily.

I wouldn't. I couldn't. Falling wasn't an option for my
poor wasted, damaged heart. It wasn't worth anything anymore. Iris deserved the world, not me.

"I can see you thinking, Jude," Iris said, pulling back
and staring down at me. "I'm not doing very well if you're
kissing me and you're busy thinking."

"Then give me something else to think about," I said,
challenging her. I hadn't felt this bold in… I didn't want
to remember when.

I didn't want to think about Grace. I didn't want to remember. I couldn't compare Iris to someone who wasn't
here.

"Still thinking," Iris said in a singsong voice and ran her
hand down my belly and cupped me. I gasped and then
I wasn't thinking about the past, I wasn't thinking about
the future, I was thinking about now, and Iris, and what
she was doing to me.

"That's more like it," I heard her say. I was too busy lost
in sensations, my skin completely on fire. "That's it," she
said, as if she was coaching me on how to give in to my
own pleasure. It was working.

"Fuck," I moaned.

"That's it, Jude, let yourself have this. Let yourself feel it." She increased the pressure with her hand and her tricky little fingers started dipping in and out of me, barely teasing my entrance.

I thought I was going to explode. I hadn't felt this way since Grace and I almost didn't want to let it happen. Would it be so wrong to enjoy this time with Iris? Would Grace hate me for this? I was so angry that I couldn't ask her.

I knew the answer to that question. No, Grace never would have hated me for anything. I missed her so fucking much, but I couldn't concentrate on her right now. I was here with Iris, and right now, all I could see was her.

"Let it happen if you want it to happen, Jude."

I was always the kind of person who tried to beat their own orgasm, to make it go longer, to make it more intense. I didn't think I could handle anything more intense than this, and she was just getting started with those little shallow thrusts with her fingers and her mouth on my neck and her other hand teasing my nipple.

I came apart, making noises I didn't know I was capable of and feeling pleasure the likes of which I had never known before. It didn't seem to end, growing and shifting, becoming sharp and then fading to more intense and warm waves as Iris told me I was so beautiful and so good.

At last the waves quieted and my body felt like it was sparkling from the inside. Iris removed her touch from between my legs and looked at my face. I gazed back at her.

"You're glowing right now," she said. "You're gorgeous."

She was grinning with the satisfaction that comes from making someone else you care about have an orgasm.

It was an intoxicating power.

"Thank you," I said because what else was I going to say?

"You're welcome, Jude. Very welcome."

We lay next to each other for a while, each basking in the afterglow of a good orgasm. Iris was tracing random shapes on my stomach, her hand going a little bit lower with each pass.

"What do you think you're doing?" I asked and she grinned up at me.

"What do you think I'm doing?" she said, pretending innocence.

"You're not doing that again. It's your turn now."

She thought about that for a second. "No. It's your turn again."

She sat up and straddled my legs.

"No, it's your turn now," I said, putting my hand on her chest. I was stronger than she was, so I could definitely pin her down on the bed, but I wasn't sure if she'd like that.

"Are you going to fight me?" I asked. There was a twinkle in her eye and I decided to go for it. I bucked my hips up and used my hands at the same time. She squealed and fell back on the bed, and I pinned her arms gently above her head. The second she told me to let go, I would.

She didn't tell me to.

"No," she said. I immediately released her wrists and she

was confused. "I meant no, I wasn't going to fight you. You can do that again. If you want."

I did. I held her wrists in one hand and leaned down to kiss her.

"I like this," she said as I kissed her deeply.

"So do I," I said. I liked having just that little bit of control. This seemed to be new for both of us. I had no idea what her sexual history was, but it didn't really matter. I didn't want to think about Iris being with other people.

I pushed my hips into hers, moving up a little bit so we were matched up. I was slightly taller, so it wasn't exact, but we got close enough.

"Fuck," she hissed through her teeth.

"More?" I asked.

"More," she said. I thrust my hips against hers and she thrust back and we started a delicate dance that increased in pace. We were both gasping and I had to reach and hold on to the bed frame.

"I'm going to come," I said.

"Me too," she said, her eyes shut as she threw her head back. I was close, but she was closer. Somehow she snuck a hand between us and maneuvered her fingers to touch me and then it was all over. I came and then she came immediately after. It was somehow just as intense as the first, lasting just as long. I collapsed on top of her, little tremors still going through me. We were both twitching and she started to laugh as I rested my head on her breast.

"That was something else," Iris said.

"It was," I agreed.

"I'm going to say something, and I do not want you to be offended. Okay?" My stomach dropped.

"What?" I said, bracing myself.

"I am so fucking hungry, I could eat my own arm." It took me a second to process her words.

"Oh. Well, let's do something about that." I got up slowly; my bones were still part liquid from coming twice in such a short time.

"No, don't leave me," she whined as she held her arms out. "Come back."

"I can't get you food and stay with you, Iris. You can't always get what you want."

She pouted adorably. "Why doesn't Salty Cove have a delivery service?" she asked.

"Because there aren't enough people to support it?" I said, pulling on a pair of shorts and tank that I usually wore around the house. I couldn't take the risk that her parents were still up and were going to look across the yard and see me naked in the kitchen. Especially since I'd just fucked their daughter. I'd probably never be able to look them in the eyes again.

I searched through the fridge and the cabinets with my sex-hazed brain. I found a few boxes of things and some cheese and apples and started making up a quick plate.

I almost jumped out of my skin when she came up behind me.

"Holy shit, Iris, you cannot do that." I turned around to find her completely naked and I forgot what I was supposed to be mad about.

"Sorry," she said, not looking all that sorry. I blinked at her and tried to remember what I was doing.

"You know your parents live right over there? And if they were in their kitchen, they could see you through that window?" I pointed the knife I'd been using to slice up some apples at the window.

Iris rolled her eyes.

"My parents are both definitely asleep, and I'm sure if they saw me, they'd think it was a dream or something. I'm not all that worried about it."

I decided to mess with her.

"Oh my god," I said, looking over at the house.

"What?" she said, diving behind me so she was completely hidden.

"Your dad is right there, getting a drink of water from the sink."

"Oh, shit, did he see me?" she asked, and I turned to see her panicking.

"No, he's not there. I just wanted to illustrate a point. You do worry about what your parents think."

Her eyes narrowed slowly. "That was mean." She stood up slowly, her eyes still darting over to the window, double-checking to make sure no one was there.

"Yes, it was, but I'm going to give you snacks."

She looked over my shoulder and made an appreciative noise. "This might do me for a few minutes."

I looked at her as I finished slicing the apples.

"We can always come back out for more." I was going

to have to stock my pantry better if she was going to need sex snacks.

"You know what I could really go for?" she asked as I held up an apple slice for her to take a bite out of.

"What?" She bit the apple. I still couldn't get over the fact Iris was here in my kitchen and she was completely naked.

"A lobster roll."

I didn't have any lobster in the house at the moment, or else I probably would have made her one.

"Is this okay for now?"

"We'll just have to do those for next time." Next time? I was still stuck on this time. I'd worry about that when the sun was in the sky. Right now it was still the night, and it was still ours.

We ate all the snacks on the tray in my new bed, with Iris lying on my legs and me leaning against the headboard.

"It's so weird that we never really had any interaction when we were in school. Four years makes a lot of difference," she said.

My parents hadn't bought this house until I'd gone into high school. We'd lived in town all during my younger years and by the time we moved, I wasn't interested in anyone or anything in this town.

"It does, when you're younger. Doesn't matter now," I said.

"Weird how things change like that." She popped a piece of cheese into her mouth and chewed.

"Come here," I said, setting the plate aside and opening

my arms to her. Iris smiled and then came to snuggle with me. She tucked her chin under my chin and I pulled the blankets over us. They were a little sweaty, but I didn't care.

It wasn't until I was waking up, the sun streaming through the curtains I'd forgotten to close, that I realized I'd fallen asleep. I couldn't remember falling asleep with such ease in…forever.

There was something different about waking up today and she was in my arms. Iris was draped on top of me, with my arm slung around her back, holding on to her as if she was a life preserver.

I was completely and utterly relaxed. I'd stopped running for a moment and it scared the shit out of me. I took a deep breath and heard a noise from Iris.

"Good morning," she said, her voice scratchy from sleep.

"Good morning," I said. I didn't know what time it was, but I had a feeling it was later than I had slept in a long time.

"You let me sleep over," she said with a soft smile.

"I didn't have much of a choice," I said.

"Ouch."

"I didn't mean it like that," I said. "Shit, what are you parents going to think?" I looked around, as if they were going to burst in the door at any moment and scream at me for sleeping with their daughter and telling me I could never see her again.

"Oh, I'm not worried," she said, stretching her arms and legs out like a cat and pointing her toes. She was somehow even more beautiful in this soft morning light, her hair tousled and her cheeks rosy and fresh, her eyes just a little puffy, but it only made her cuter.

"What?" Iris asked and I realized I'd been staring at her.

"You're so pretty," I said, brushing some hair behind her ear. She blushed and pulled the blanket up to hide her face, but I held it so she couldn't.

"Stop it," she whined. "I look like crap. I can feel it." If this was looking like crap, then she should look like crap every day.

"You don't, I promise. I don't give compliments if I don't mean them." What use was there in blowing smoke up someone's ass?

"Whatever," she said, rolling her eyes. "I need to pee and brush my teeth. Do you have anything I could do that with?"

"I mean, there's a toilet right there, but you could always just go out to the trees, as long as you check for Larry first." She stared at me for a second, confused, and then burst out laughing as she slid out of bed and I got to bask in the glory of her body in the sunshine.

"Toothbrush. Do you have another toothbrush?"

I grinned at her. "Yeah, under the sink. You can use my floss or toothpaste or whatever. Help yourself." No one had ever been in my bathroom, which was a strange realization. I'd isolated myself so completely and totally, and now I was out of practice with being a host. I hoped she didn't mind my fumblings as I got used to being around other humans again.

"Thanks," she said, grabbing my tank and shorts from

the night before and putting them on. The shorts were long for her, but they hugged her ass in such a wonderful way, I would have collapsed if I hadn't already been lying down.

"You can keep the clothes," I blurted out as my eyes traveled upward to see how her chest filled out the tank.

"I'm not sure if I should wear this shirt in public," she said, pointing at her protruding nipples and the way that both her breasts were threatening to spill out the sides.

"No, you might cause too many car crashes and accidents. Best to only wear it in my house." Her eyes narrowed and she headed to the bathroom, shutting the door. I lay back on the bed and stared at the ceiling. I should get up and make some food, or do something. I also had to pee, though, so I found some other clothes and headed to one of the other bathrooms in the house. When I was headed back to the master bedroom, I saw Iris in the kitchen, still wearing my clothes. According to the microwave, it was just after seven. She was digging in the fridge.

"What are you looking for?"

"I'm not sure. I know we had that plate, but that was like hours ago. I need something else and I don't want to face my parents yet, so." She stood up and shrugged, holding a carton of eggs.

"I can make you breakfast. I don't mind. What would you like?"

"I'm not picky."

She handed me the eggs. I pushed her into a chair and told her that I would handle it.

"One of these days I'm going to make up for all those

meals you've made me," she said. "I'm going to cook for you, Jude Wicks. And it's going to blow your mind."

"I'm looking forward to that," I said, and I was. I let myself have a moment of picturing Iris in the kitchen, making something and singing to a Dolly Parton song, while Dolly Parton the dog sat at her feet, hoping for scraps.

That wasn't what this was about. This was supposed to be just sex, but it had turned into sex, and then sleeping and cuddling, and then breakfast. I opened my mouth to tell her that we should stop, but then I looked at her and I couldn't. Plus, I was hungry.

I whipped up cheese and pepper omelets and threw some frozen hash browns in a pan.

"Coffee?" Iris said in a whiny voice. "Coffeeeeeeee."

I pointed to the coffee maker. One of my dreams—when I'd allowed myself to have dreams—had been to get a real espresso maker for my home so I could make real coffee drinks at home and maybe even have coffee parties. Grace would've liked that idea.

I wouldn't allow myself to think about her when I was with Iris.

"Do you have any cream or anything?"

"I've got heavy cream in the fridge and some milk."

"Fuck yeah, heavy cream sounds good." She was so enthusiastic about the strangest things.

"I'll have some too," I said, even though I always took mine black. The two of us sat together at the table and ate our omelets, each lost in our thoughts.

"Okay, what are you thinking? You haven't thrown me

out and you made me breakfast, but what about every-thing else?" she asked. One of her feet was jiggling under the table.

"I'm thinking that we need to set some better bound-aries because right now, it doesn't feel like there are any." I didn't want to say them, but they needed to be said. Some-one had to be the voice of reason. This thing was never going to go anywhere, and it would be wrong of me to get her hopes up and string her along.

"Okay. What kind of boundaries do you want to set? You can set yours and I'll set mine." Good, she was on board with this. That was a relief. I didn't know if she was going to be okay with that. I didn't want this to end, but I didn't want to get in too deep and then end up with Iris getting her heart broken.

"I think we should spend less time together if we're going to do this 'just sex' thing. It muddies the waters. So on nights when we're going to be together, I think we should have a buffer. You can come over when you want, we'll do all that stuff and then you can either stay the night or go home. I think we should sleep in separate rooms if you stay over. I know that sounds mean, but I'm only doing it because I think it's for the best. I don't want to hurt you."

Her face fell, but then she put on a cheerful (and fake) smile.

"No, yeah, that's good. I can do that. How about I text or call you before I'm going to come over instead of just showing up? Then you can say yes or no, depending on how you feel." Her tone wasn't enthusiastic.

"Great," I said, even though my stomach twisted a little.

We talked about other things, but we agreed that we still would spend non-sex time together, but no kissing, no touching.

"So are you saying you want to have sex with me again?" she said.

"That's a definite yes, Iris," I said. "Is there a word that means more than yes? Because whatever that is, that's how much I want to have sex with you again."

She laughed a little. "I'm sure there's one in German."

"Well, if you figure it out, then let me know." I took the dishes to the sink and rinsed them off before putting them in the dishwasher.

Iris looked out the window at her parents' house.

"Okay, I guess I should grow up and go see my parents. I also really miss Dolly. Would you mind if I brought her with me sometimes?"

"No, not at all. If you want, we can order her a bed, so she'll have someplace to sleep." I'd already bought some bowls for her, but hadn't told Iris about that. I needed to get some food from her as well. This was completely in contrast to the rules we'd just made, but I was going to ignore that right now.

I didn't want her to leave either. I pretended to be busy in the kitchen as she got dressed and tried to make it look like she hadn't been fucking all night.

"Presentable?" she said. "I never thought I would have to do a walk of shame in front of my parents." She made a face. "Ugh, I hate that term. There's nothing shameful about consensual fucking." She looked gorgeous and all I wanted to do was pick her up and throw her back into bed again. I clenched my hands behind my back so I wouldn't.

"You're right. No shame in our game." It was corny, but I found myself feeling increasingly goofy around her. Feeling silly and a little carefree again. I shouldn't let it happen, but there wasn't much to be done about it now. My heart, this hard, broken thing, was starting to open again by being around Iris. I knew it needed to stop, but I didn't know how. Grace's laugh echoed in the back of my mind. I remembered the person I had been with her and I was starting to feel like that woman again. At this point, I didn't know if I could stop the transformation back, or if I even wanted to.

Iris didn't kiss me goodbye, and when she left, our goodbye felt unfinished. Incomplete. Missing something.

For a second, I almost called at her as she walked across the yard and back up the porch to her parents' house.

I kept my mouth shut and went back into the house alone.

Chapter Thirteen

Iris

Walking back over to my parents' house felt like an eternity. I hadn't kissed Jude goodbye, and I think I would have felt better if I'd had that little bit of luck to go with me. I'd woken up in the middle of the night to use the bathroom and had gotten out of bed so carefully to avoid waking Jude. I hadn't needed to worry. She was completely out, even snoring slightly. The tension was gone from her face in sleep. I'd sat on the edge of the bed for a moment, watching her.

I knew what had happened last night. I knew that something had completely changed between us and no matter what I said about keeping this only physical, my heart and feelings were completely and totally involved.

I'd been naïve to think I could do this without completely falling for her.

If I was being truthful with myself, I already had and just hadn't realized it yet.

I'd snuggled back into bed with her, lying across her fabulous chest and wrapping my arm around her. I couldn't remember the last time I'd slept like this with another person. It was so warm and comfortable and I wanted every night to be like this.

I wanted to be with Jude. I wanted everything.

She didn't have everything to give me, but that didn't matter. I'd take what I could get because it was better than having everything with someone else. I knew that with complete certainty in every cell of my body.

I would shut my mouth and take what I could get as long as she would give it to me. If that was forever, so be it. I was in. I was all the way in.

I wouldn't say that she completely broke my heart when she wanted to set boundaries, but if that was what she needed to do, that was what she needed. We could be careful with each other.

I opened the door and walked in to a regular morning.

Dolly raced to see me. "Hey, I missed you. Have you been a good girl?" She licked my face and wiggled around in happiness.

"She was good, but we weren't expecting to be dog sitting, Iris," Mom said, coming out of the kitchen while drying her hands on a dish towel.

"Yeah, sorry about that. It was completely unplanned."

I finally looked up at her and I couldn't read the look in her eyes.

"Did you patch things up with Jude?" she asked, and there was no mistaking the unspoken question.

"Something like that," I said, standing up. "Do you mind if I take a shower?"

I didn't normally ask permission, but I wanted to tread lightly right now until I knew what their stance on me having casual sex was.

"Sure, go ahead."

I scurried to the bathroom and stripped off my clothes from the day before. Had it really been less than a day that Jude had picked me up on her motorcycle and taken me for a ride to the beach?

After my shower, I went to my room and got dressed and then decided to get it over with.

"Okay, what do you want to know?" I said when I came back out.

Mom was on the couch sipping some tea and Dad wasn't reading anymore.

"What is your relationship with Jude?" Mom asked as I sat down next to her.

"Uh, not sure right now. It's a little up in the air." I just hoped they weren't going to give me a safe sex talk. The last time around they had assumed that I was going to be sleeping with a cis boy, so they hadn't really covered sex with someone like Jude. That was fine. I could figure it out on my own.

My parents didn't seem too happy with my relationship, but they didn't stop me from going over to Jude's and staying the night for the next two weeks. I didn't go every night, of course, but I would text her after work, or she'd message me and ask if I wanted to come over. I was doing okay at keeping things on the physical side only, but the more I spent time naked with her, the more my feelings were continuing to grow in a way that completely scared the shit out of me. When I'd seen her that first night, there was a hard shell around her and now that shell was breaking, revealing someone soft and funny and vulnerable. Plus, the sex? The sex was phenomenal.

Jude and I would lie in bed and talk about plot holes in movies and she showed me her crochet projects and told me stories of the other fishermen. She'd started hanging out with a few of them after she got off in the morning, and once she'd even had coffee with Kenny and Travis. I'd seen them all at The Lobster Pot and knew they were good guys. I was glad Jude was making friends. I'd been back to the queer group again, and I was still on the fence about Marina, but I'd definitely become friends with more than a few people in the group. Things had changed in Salty Cove since I'd left, even more than I knew.

One night my parents sat me down again. They hadn't made a peep about me seeing Jude again after the first few questions, so I was a little confused at first.

"Be careful with Jude, Iris. She's been through something," Dad said after sharing a look with Mom.

"What do you mean?" I said. Did they know what had happened with Jude? Had they known this whole time and hadn't said anything to me?

"She lost someone. We don't know all the details, but it was bad. Car accident."

Oh. That...explained a lot. That explained pretty much everything.

"Do you know anything else?" I asked.

"Just that Jude's parents didn't seem to care as much as they should have. They acted like she'd just lost a friend, and not a person who meant everything to her. Never liked those people," Dad said.

"Me neither," Mom agreed. "You really should talk to Jude about it. And be careful with yourself. I don't want my daughter to have a broken heart, okay, baby girl?" She gave me a stern look as if I could prevent the breaking of my own heart.

"Yeah, sure. I'll do my best." They let me digest that for a few moments.

"You okay?" Mom asked.

"Yeah, fine, just thinking about a lot. I need to talk to Jude."

"I think that's a good idea," Dad said.

I spent the rest of the day cleaning and thinking about Jude. I kept looking over at her house and wondering what she was doing, since her motorcycle was gone. I knew I needed to give her time and space, but I didn't want to give her time and space. That might mean that she would think about things and change her mind.

That would completely devastate me. A month ago, I hadn't thought about Jude Wicks even once, and now she was as integral to my life as Dolly and my parents. I hadn't meant for it to happen, but it had, and now I was basically fucked. Sure, I was sticking around for a while, but if things went south with Jude, I didn't see myself being able to stay after that. Then I'd be running back to Boston. I'd been doing a lot of running lately and I didn't want to have to do any more.

To keep my mind off things, I started looking up real estate stuff online. Mom had suggested that I take classes, which were held at my old high school on Thursday nights, so I signed up to start the next session in two weeks and ordered my books. I couldn't do much else, so I ended up falling into a hole of reading real estate listings for other Maine towns and then looking at the worst interior shots. If you want to sell your house, you could maybe clean it before you take pictures?

My parents still weren't back by the afternoon, so their impromptu date must have been going well. Getting an idea, I hopped in my car with Dolly and headed to the bigger town next to Salty Cove and the small organic market to get something to make for my parents for dinner. I might as well make them a nice dinner for when they got back.

I saw at least three people I went to high school with, including Marina and Jace, doing their weekly shopping.

"Oh, hey," I said when I nearly walked into their cart.

"Hey," she said. "Are you willing to make small talk with me?" She let out a little nervous laugh and Jace seemed really interested in the ceiling tiles of the store.

"I guess. I'm still working on that forgiveness, though."

"Fair enough. Listen, if you ever want to hang out, this is an open invitation. Coffee, whatever." She pulled out a business card and handed it to me.

"I'll think about it." I slid the card into my wallet and pushed my cart down the aisle.

Who knew that I would be having a civil conversation with Marina after high school? I did not have that one on my Bingo card. Shaking my head, I picked up some chicken, summer squash, spinach, mozzarella, tomatoes, basil, and a few spices that my parents didn't already have.

My dad had a small propane grill that he used and he'd shown me how ages ago. I thought I could handle it, so I hauled it out, got it going, and started marinating the chicken.

Just before six my parents arrived back at home. I was in the kitchen chopping the squash to put on skewers to add next to the chicken on the grill. Jude still wasn't back yet. I couldn't stop flinching at every single sound of a motor, waiting to hear the telltale rumble.

"How was your date?" I asked as I opened up the grill to put the chicken on.

Mom and Dad were both grinning and no joke, they held hands as they walked up on the porch and over to me.

"It was lovely," Mom said. She was beaming and it made me want to cry.

"What's happening here?" Dad asked.

"Making dinner," I said. "Hope you're hungry. This should be done pretty soon." I was feeling pretty good about my day, but I still couldn't stop thinking about Jude. I wanted to see her tonight.

"I'm so spoiled," Mom said, putting both hands on my shoulders and kissing my cheek.

"You should be spoiled," I said. "You really should, Mom. I know I don't say it enough, but thank you. For everything."

Tears sparkled in her eyes and she gave me a big hug. "You're welcome, baby girl. Anything for you." I finished up the chicken and brought everything inside.

"You want to invite Jude?" Dad asked.

"She's not home, and even if she was, that would be weird," I said.

"Why would it be weird? She's been here before," Mom said, sitting down as I put some chicken and squash on her plate. I'd already put the salads on separate plates.

Dad fussed about eating salad, but he ended up loving it.

"How about this: once a week I'll take care of dinner. Either I'll bring something home from work, or I'll cook." I expected my mom to protest, but she didn't.

Wow, that must have been some date they went on.

We finished dinner and I did the dishes as well. I almost

dropped a plate in the sink when I heard the motorcycle pull into the driveway. There she was. I ducked down so she wouldn't catch me staring at her as she got off the bike.

"I'm going to go talk to her," I said, drying my hands on a dish towel that had autumn leaves on it.

"You sure that's a good idea?" Mom asked.

"Yeah, it'll be fine. I need to talk to her. I'll take Dolly this time, in case I don't come back tonight," I said.

Mom and Dad shared a look and I thought one or both of them was going to protest, but Dad shrugged and Mom heaved a sigh.

"Be careful" was all she said.

"I will."

I knocked on the door and waited on the porch. That seemed like the right thing to do instead of walking right in. I wasn't going to just attack her with questions, even though that was all I wanted to talk to her about. I wanted to give her room to talk. I also really wanted to have sex with her again, and that was warring with my curiosity and might be winning the battle for what I wanted first. Truth or sex? Right now I was thinking sex.

The door opened and there was Jude.

"Hey, I brought Dolly so my parents wouldn't have to watch her," I said as Dolly sprinted into the house and headed for the new couch.

"That's fine," she said. "What about food for her? Will she be okay?"

I held up the bag of dog food I'd brought. "She'll be fine."

"I got her some bowls last week, they're in the kitchen."

I followed her to the little area she'd set up for Dolly. There was already water in the bowl. Like she'd been expecting us. That made my heart swell a little bit.

"I got her a bed too," she said, showing me the little spot in the living room where she'd gotten a dark gray dog bed for Dolly.

"What's all this?" There were toys as well that Dolly hadn't noticed yet, or else she would have been all over them.

"I figured if she was going to be around, I should make her comfortable."

I had to not look at her or I might have started crying. It was just so sweet. "Thank you, this is amazing," I said, my voice a little choked.

"Hey," she said, touching my shoulder and making me face her. I wasn't crying, but the tears were ready and waiting.

"What is it?" she said, rubbing my shoulder.

"I'm fine. This is just really nice. Thank you." I wiped a few tears and Jude did something that only made my emotions worse: she hugged me.

We hadn't talked about hugs being part of the rules, but I hoped they were allowed because Jude was a great hugger. Her arms were so strong that I let myself go, and I knew that when I was in the circle of her arms, nothing could hurt me. I was protected, except from one thing: Jude.

The hug didn't last as long as I wanted it to, and she pulled back and wiped my eyes.

"It's not a big deal," she said, brushing the kindness off.

"It is a big deal. I promise."

A squeaking noise made both of us turn—Dolly had found the toys.

"You got her squeaky toys?" I asked. I had gotten rid of all of them after the first two weeks of having Dolly, or at least hid them when she wasn't looking.

"Yeah, why?"

I groaned. "Because now that's the only sound we're going to hear for the foreseeable future. She gets obsessed with one toy and will only play with that one for days and days and days. She'll rip it to shreds and then be on to the next one."

Jude looked at Dolly, who was running around and squeaking and the happiest dog to ever exist.

"Should we take it away from her? I feel bad now."

"No, but let's gather up the others, if there are any." While Dolly ran around squeaking the toy, we went through the others and found a few more noisy offenders. Jude put them in the back of the cabinet in the kitchen.

"Do you want anything to eat?" she asked. "I went shopping today and got a few things."

"Is that allowed?" I asked.

"What do you mean?"

"With the rules? Is food allowed?" I was partly joking, but partly serious. We had set some parameters, but there was still a lot of gray area that I wasn't sure about.

"Yes, food is allowed. I'm not that much of a monster."

I leaned my head on her shoulder.

"You're not even a little bit of a monster. I know you think you are, but you're not." I waited for her to argue, but she didn't.

The house was quiet except for the toy. I hoped Dolly would wear herself out at some point.

"Do you want a drink?" she asked.

"Sure, why not?" She got out a bottle of some wine and poured us both glasses. "This is fancy," I said. "No beer?"

"You don't like beer," she said.

"Yeah, but you do." I sipped the wine. It was sweet and rich.

"I can learn to like this," she said, taking a cautious sip and then making a face. I laughed.

"I'll drink the wine, you can get a beer. Have what you want, Jude. You should always have what you want." She set the glass down and I poured what was left of it in my glass.

Jude popped the top on a beer and took a sip, sighing in relief.

"Better?" I asked.

"Much," she said. I wasn't sure what to do now. Did we just drink and then...what? I was bad at initiating sex, apparently. I wasn't sure if she even wanted to have sex tonight. That hadn't been discussed.

Yet.

"Something wrong?" she asked, leaning against the counter and nursing her beer. I gulped the wine, needing a little liquid courage.

"No, I'm just wondering, um, how the night is going to go? We talked about boundaries, but we didn't really talk about how this is going to go. I mean, I assume that since you said I could come over, you were up for stuff, but…" I trailed off. I could feel my face getting completely and totally red.

Jude set her beer down and walked toward me.

"What do you want out of tonight?" she asked, leaning closer. The warmth from her skin radiated over me.

"I just want you," I said, telling the truth.

"You can have me any way you want me."

"Any way?" I asked, raising my eyebrows.

"Within reason. And I definitely don't ever want to do anything that involves sex and electricity." My eyes went wide. I mean, I'd heard about that kind of thing, but that wasn't anything I was into either.

"So that's a no to hooking your nipples up to a car battery and zapping you?"

She laughed softly. "That's a definite no."

I wanted to know what she would say yes to.

"Right now I'd love to watch you undress, and then let me kiss you all over," she said.

"Can I bring my wine?" I asked. I headed back to Jude's bedroom, hoping she would follow.

She did.

"Can you undress and hold that at the same time?" she asked and I looked at her as if she had lost her mind.

"How coordinated do you think I am?" I asked, setting the wine down on the only flat surface that wasn't the bed, aka, the floor. We still had to get some more furniture for the bedroom. And paint. We needed to paint. That would come. I was determined to redo this entire house, down to the bathrooms.

"You seem pretty graceful to me," she said, and I knew that was a lie, but whatever. I'd take a compliment where I could get it.

"I'll get naked if you do one thing for me," I said as I started to pull my shirt over my head.

She leaned back on the bed as if she was enjoying the show. "What's that?"

I pulled my shirt over my head and tossed it into the corner of the room. "If you get naked too."

"I guess I can do that," she said, sitting up and pulling off her own shirt. No bra again. I was momentarily unable to think as I stared.

"Keep going," she urged me as I remembered I was supposed to be getting naked. Right. Clothes off.

I thought about making it sexy, but things between us were still so new that we didn't need the seduction. We needed to get naked as soon as possible to get down to business. The seduction would come later. Right now it was all about desperate need.

"Turn around," Jude said once I was completely divested of my clothing. The room was a little chilly, but it wasn't going to stay that way.

I twirled slowly, feeling completely exposed, but I guess that was the point.

"You're so beautiful, Iris. So fucking beautiful, come here."

I looked at her over my shoulder and our eyes locked and I swear, I burst into flames. "Take off your pants."

She didn't have anything on top, but her shorts were still on. She lifted her hips and got everything off at once, throwing them and then smirking at me.

"Happy?"

"With you naked? Fuck yeah." I stood next to the bed and she reached for me.

"I need you," she said and I melted. I crawled on top of her and we started kissing, our bodies tangling together as we rolled and kissed and gasped and tasted one another. My hands got busy and her hands got busy, and it was a struggle to see who was going to come first as we kissed and our hands stroked and teased.

I was the first one to come, but she followed and then we were off to the races. I lost count of how many times I came, how many times she came, and how many ways we found to pleasure each other. Some worked, some didn't. Some we tried and halfway through abandoned. Some were very, very good.

"I can't come any more right now," I said, my chest heaving as sweat dripped down my body. We were going to have to change the sheets, that was for sure.

"Me neither," she said, staring at the ceiling. Her hair was all over the place and her cheeks were flushed, as well as her chest. I couldn't stop staring at her incredible body. I got to fuck that body and bring it to orgasm. This was the best night of my life.

A squeaking sound interrupted our afterglow.

"I'm going to murder that toy," I said. "Or at least it's going to have an unfortunate accident."

Jude laughed and sat up.

"What are you doing tomorrow?" she asked.

"I don't have to work until four," I said. "Why?"

"Do you want to come to work with me?"

Was she serious?

"Like, on the boat and everything?"

"Yeah. I have extra gear. And I could use a pair of hands to help me out." If she'd asked me a few weeks ago, I probably would have said no, but now...

"What time do we have to get up?"

"Four thirty."

I groaned. "Fuck me, that's early, Jude."

"I'll make you tons and tons of coffee and take you out for brunch after. Anything you want." Free food was tempting. So tempting. Plus, there was the chance to spend time with Jude.

"Okay?"

"You don't sound so sure about that," Jude said.

"No, I'll do it. I just... I'll need a nap in the afternoon. I think I can swing it." I was already tired and boneless from the sex and now I was going to do a ton of physical work at the crack of dawn and then have a shift at The Lobster Pot. But I was going to suck it up and do it.

For Jude. Only for Jude. I must love her.

The thought was so casual and so easy, I didn't realize that I'd thought it for a few moments. I gasped, as if I'd said it out loud.

"What?" Jude said, looking around.

"Nothing," I said. "I just forgot to do something."

Holy shit, I loved Jude. Like, completely and totally. Wanted to spend the rest of my life making her happy, waking up next to her, listening to her snore, fighting with her about what movie to watch, shopping for towels kind of love.

I wanted it all, even if that meant I had to get used to the smell of bait.

Because I loved her.

I loved Jude Wicks and I could never let her find out because I'd broken the ultimate rule. We'd agreed this would just be physical and bam, I broke the main rule. It wasn't my heart's fault. I mean, how could I not fall in love with her? It was an inevitable conclusion to me moving next door. It was going to happen whether I meant it to or not. From that first glance of her through the window and here I was. In love.

"Are you sure you're okay?" she said.

"Yup," I squeaked just like Dolly's toy. "But I think I'm going to need a shower and we need to change the sheets and maybe a snack before some sleep seeing as how we have to be awake in a few hours. Someone made me agree to go out on a boat before the sun comes up." I leaned over and spanked her ass and she yelped, but there was a little sound of pleasure in it too.

"Can I join you in the shower? We should conserve water." She said it with a serious face.

"Oh, well, we want to be environmentally conscious. It's

really important these days." I nodded and she followed me into the attached bathroom where I turned the shower on.

"Did I really agree to go on the boat with you tomorrow?" I said as we waited for the water to warm up.

"Yes, you did. No backing out now, Iris."

I groaned and she pushed me into the shower.

Four thirty came way too early. Like seriously early. So fucking early. I swatted at Jude's hand as she tried to shake me awake.

"Fuck no," I said, burying my face into the pillow. The room was still dark and it was still night as far as I was concerned.

"If I show you my boobs, will you get up?"

I lifted my head and squinted through one eye to see if she was actually serious. "Show me," I said, rolling over onto my back. I hadn't gotten nearly enough sleep, but I would suck it up if it meant I got to see her breasts.

Jude pulled her shirt over her head in the process of getting dressed.

"There you go. Now you have to get up."

I moaned, but slid to the floor and stood up. "Why did I agree to this?" I said. Oh, right, because I was in love with her, which she didn't know and I didn't plan on telling her about.

"I don't know. I didn't think you would," Jude said, putting on some thick work pants.

"Do you have clothes for me?" The jeans and tank I'd

brought to put on for what I thought would be a regular day weren't going to cut it out on the ocean.

"Yeah, you can borrow anything of mine."

Since she was a little taller, her pants were too long, so I rolled them up, and she put a long-sleeved shirt on me. Had to roll the sleeves up too.

"I look ridiculous," I said as I checked myself out in the bathroom mirror as she brushed her teeth.

"You look hot," she said through a mouthful of toothpaste.

"I do not," I said. The clothes were just baggy enough to look ridiculous.

She spit in the sink and wiped her mouth.

"Yeah, you do," she said, pulling me close and kissing me. It was early, but the kiss woke me right up and I was ready to say fuck fishing and take her back to bed. The clothes that were too baggy on me were really working for her and I didn't want to keep my hands off her.

Jude made a sound of pleasure and then broke the kiss.

"I thought kissing wasn't allowed," I said.

"Rules have changed" was her answer. Okay then. "Come on, we have to get going."

She left the bathroom and I yelled that I needed coffee.

After I had sucked down at least one cup, Jude made some more for me to take with us. I dropped Dolly off next door where no one was awake and then Jude handed me my helmet.

"Do we have to take the bike?" I asked. I didn't fancy riding on the cold roads in the dark this early.

"We don't have to," she said, but she was practically pouting, so I sucked it up and put on the helmet. Because I loved her.

Chapter Fourteen

Jude

I could tell she definitely wasn't into this, but she was going along with it. Even when we got into the dinghy and it rocked back and forth and she helped me row out to the boat, and when she had to smell the bait and the diesel from the engine. I'd gotten so used to those scents that I'd forgotten how intense they were the first few times.

It was like I'd been asleep for two years and now I was waking up. Everything was brighter, more intense. Or maybe that was Iris. She'd burst into my life and nothing was the same. I'd fought it, but not very hard, apparently. Over these past few weeks of trying to have purely a physical relationship, something in me had shifted. I still thought about Grace. I still missed her terribly, but I let myself have moments of joy. Moments of joy with someone else. Something told me that she would be pleased that I could laugh with someone else. I'd spent two years mourning her and what had it gotten me? Nothing. A whole lot of misery and anger and bitterness. Grace wouldn't have wanted that. She wouldn't have wanted me to cut myself off from life like some sort of martyr. In fact, I could picture her yelling at me. Grace hadn't yelled often, so when she did, people paid attention.

We'd agreed to just have a physical relationship and now here she was wrinkling her nose at the bait barrel and drinking all my coffee. I didn't mind.

Work was a little more difficult that morning, and I wasn't used to talking to another person while I went about my day, but it was exciting to see her wonder and her enthusiasm for helping me. She learned quickly, and made sure to listen to me when I told her how to be safe on the boat and with the equipment.

"Bye bye, tiny lobster," she said, holding up a male lobster that was too small to keep.

"Do you have to say goodbye to all of them?" I asked. She was slowing up the process considerably.

"I have to wish them well. Farewell, tiny lobster. Let's hope you don't end up in a trap when you get bigger." She tossed it over the side and gave a little wave.

"Do you want to try?" I asked, showing her how to put the rubber bands on the claws so you didn't get your fingers pinched off. It took some finesse, and the lobsters could snap and twist if you didn't hold them just right. Several of them ended up flopping around on the deck of the boat and we had to go chasing them down.

"I don't normally run this much on my boat," I said, leaning against the side and catching my breath.

"I'm sorry, but I don't know how you smell this every day," she said, gagging at the bait barrel.

"You get used to it somehow," I said. "Let's take a break." I took off my gloves. The sun had finally come up and it was a lot warmer on the water. It was shaping up to be a gorgeous day.

I leaned on the side of the boat and she came to lean next to me.

"I'm sweating under here," she said, taking off her jacket. "I don't know how you do this every day. Holy shit, Jude. No wonder your arms are like that. You know, you could probably sell this to rich people as some sort of new workout. LobFit or something. Make more money."

I laughed because that wasn't a horrible idea. There were tourists who would pay to come out on boats and get the "Maine experience." It was an idea. I didn't think I could fish full time for much longer. It had served its purpose, but I was ready for something else. I didn't know if that coincided with Iris coming back, or if it was just a natural evolution. I was ready to start waking up again.

I'd fought to stay numb for so long and I'd worked so hard at it that letting myself feel again wasn't easy. I was going to have to take it a little at a time and it was time to talk to Iris about Grace.

"I came back because my girlfriend died," I blurted out. That wasn't how I'd intended to tell her, but once the words were out, it was like a dam had been opened. I'd been holding on to it so hard, making it a part of myself and my story and my life. Now it was time to let it go.

She hugged me, which I didn't expect. It threw me off balance for a second. Her hair smelled like my shampoo.

"I'm so sorry," she said, and I let the tears that I'd been ignoring for two years spill from my eyes. I cried hard. I sobbed and my chest heaved and I couldn't breathe and I didn't know how long it went on for, but she held me. She held me and let me ugly cry on her shoulder with snot coming out of my nose and spit and all the pain that came from inside me. It was like cutting a vein and letting everything bleed out.

"It's okay," she kept saying. "It's okay."

After ten minutes or three hours the sobs subsided into hiccups and she wiped my eyes with her fingers. I still had my gloves on and they were covered in all manner of gross things.

"Thank you for telling me. You don't have to say anything else if you don't want to." I did.

"We met in college and she lived down the hall. The moment I saw her it was just…magic. She was magic. She was also difficult and moody and silly and sweet and everything. She was my everything and then one night she was driving and we don't really know what happened, but she was gone. My Grace was gone."

I told Iris all about Grace: the day we met, what she

said, our first date, the day we'd moved in together, our first huge fight. I told her so many things about Grace and she listened. I told her about the little ways she reminded me of Grace: her stubbornness, her love for her family, her sense of humor.

"Our first date was at a bar and there was a live band playing sea shanties. She made a gagging noise and rolled her eyes and asked if I wanted to go somewhere else, and it was like I knew she was going to be a huge part of my life. I don't think we spent much time apart from then on, and then we traveled everywhere and slept under the stars and put up with gross apartments. Grace had never been to Salty Cove, but I knew she would have loved it."

She heard it all and held me so tight, this incredible girl that I didn't deserve. I broke in that moment, but it wasn't breaking apart. It was coming together. I trembled at the thought, but it felt right. Everything with Iris had felt right.

"She sounds amazing," Iris said and there wasn't a hint of jealousy in her tone.

"She was. She was just…she was my Grace." I could see her face in my mind in complete and perfect detail. She didn't look anything like Iris, but she did remind me of her in some ways. I think they would have gotten along.

"I knew there was something painful in your life, Jude, but I didn't know the extent of it. I'm sorry she was taken from you." I was still so angry about that. About the fact that she hadn't gotten to live her life. The emotions after her death had been too much, so I'd cut myself off from everything. Came back to Salty Cove and hibernated for two years. Until Iris.

When I'd met her, I'd come alive. I'd woken up. I didn't know what this new world without Grace was going to hold for me, but I was finally ready to find out.

"Did you ever talk to anyone?" Iris asked.

"Yeah, I had a therapist for a while, but I didn't want to feel anything, and talking made me feel things, so I stopped. Maybe I'll start up again. Find someone here." It was an idea.

"I'm not saying you have to, if you don't want to." She rested her hands on my shoulders and I put my hands on her waist.

"I know. I should. I have no problems with therapy."

We swayed with the rocking of the boat. I was glad she hadn't gotten seasick.

"How long are you going to stay?" I asked.

"How long do you want me to stay?" she asked and I took a breath before I said the words that completely scared the shit out of me.

"Forever. Stay with me forever."

Tears glistened in the corners of her eyes.

"Are you sure?" Her voice cracked.

"Yes. Stay with me."

"Good, because I'm going to tell you something and I don't want you to flip out." I braced myself, even though I had an inkling what it could be. "I know it's against the rules, but we've basically broken all of them already. I love you, Jude. A lot. Like, more than all the drops in this entire ocean. So much that it scares me and I know you probably aren't ready to hear it, but I have to say it."

The words tumbled out all at once and I could tell she was terrified. Her hands trembled on my shoulders, even through the thick material of my shirt and coat.

"I love you, Iris. I know it's too soon and I know it's too much, but it's true. And I feel like I'm betraying Grace and that sucks, but I love you anyway." The tears were back for both of us so we clung to each other as the water rose and fell under the boat. Our footing might be unsteady, but we clung to each other as anchors.

"I can't believe you love me," she said. "After everything and just... Why me?"

I pulled back so I could look at her face, which was blotchy and beautiful.

I pulled off my gloves so I could touch her skin. Her nose was running a little and I could feel the remnants of salt from her tears and the ocean spray.

"Because you're everything I need. Because you're so kind, and beautiful and chaotic and bright and bold. You're what I want to be, but could never be. You make me want to wake up in the morning. You make me want to live and breathe again. Being with you feels like taking a deep breath for the first time." I couldn't put it any other way.

"That's the nicest thing anyone has ever said to me," she said, wiping her nose on her sleeve. "Sorry, I'll wash this before I give it back to you."

I laughed. "There's a lot more stuff than snot on that shirt, so I'm not worried."

That made her giggle. "Don't make me think about that, please. I'm trying not to let myself get nauseated by the bait." The barrel was pretty close to us.

"Come on," I said, walking her toward the wheel. "I'm going to teach you how to steer the boat." I put her in front of me so I was behind her. I spoke in her ear and felt her trembling against me.

"I'm afraid I'm going to crash with you standing right there like that."

"I won't let you crash," I said. "Promise."

She looked over her shoulder at me. "Because you love me?"

I kissed her cheek. "That water is also really cold and I don't feel like going for a dip or losing my catch for today." Iris narrowed her eyes at me. "But it's mostly because I love you."

"You're lucky I love you back or else I might be offended."

We got through the rest of my traps with no incident, but it took two more hours to do it with Iris's help than when I did it alone. I didn't tell her that.

By the time we made it back to the dock, we were both so hungry we considered eating the raw lobsters. I said hello to Kenny and asked how his wife was doing, since she was pregnant with their third child. He grunted and then I introduced Iris around and she charmed them all, joking about the names of the boats and asking them funny questions. I watched her and fell even deeper.

I still loved Grace, yes, but I could love in two directions. My love for Grace would last, but my love for Iris was here and now. They weren't mutually exclusive.

After we hung out with a few of the guys, we showered off and ran into Cindy on our way back to my bike.

"Hello, nice to see you two together," she said and there was a heavy hint of what she was leaving unsaid.

"I'll see you in a few hours," Iris said.

"Have fun," she said, giving me a wink. "Nice to see you, Jude."

Iris looked at me after Cindy had gone back upstairs to the restaurant.

"Welp, everyone else is going to know that I rode your motorcycle," Iris said.

"Is that what the kids are calling it these days?" I said and she burst out laughing.

"If not, then they should."

We ended up at the local tiny diner that made all its bread and pastries on the premises by a woman who everyone considered their grandmother.

"I get to have whatever I want, right?" Iris said, scanning the menu.

"Whatever you want," I said, and I wasn't just talking about breakfast. I'd give her anything she wanted. I'd give her everything she wanted.

I hadn't been lying when I'd told her that it was easier to breathe around her. Letting someone know about Grace had untied a knot inside me that I'd been clinging to. It had served me for those two years while I waited in limbo. I didn't have any regrets about those years. I didn't think they were wasted. I think I needed them to get to this place, and I was going to need more years ahead. To grieve. To heal. To find out how to live again.

I was going to learn how to live again with Iris.

Iris got biscuits and gravy and grits and hash browns and fruit and one chocolate chip pancake.

"I am weak from hunger," she said while we waited for our food to come. I'd ordered the biscuits and gravy as well, along with bacon and three scrambled eggs.

"You'll survive."

She rested her head on her arms on the table. "I don't know how you do this every day. I really don't." She yawned.

"I know. I'm not going to do it so much anymore. I'm going to find other ways to make money that don't isolate me so much." Plus, it really was dangerous to go out alone. I hadn't cared before, but I had someone who cared about what happened to me now.

"Good, that means you can spend more time with me," she said, leaning her chin on my shoulder and grinning at me.

"Hey, guess what?" she said.

"What?" I asked.

"I love you."

"I love you," I said, and it didn't feel wrong saying it. It felt nothing but right.

"You can always talk about Grace with me, you know.

I want you to be able to, because she's part of you, even if she's not here anymore."

What had I done to deserve two incredible women in my life? You just didn't get more than one soul mate. No one was that lucky. Love had been taken away from me once, and I couldn't spend my time with Iris worrying about if I was going to lose her or not, even when my anxiety screamed at me that something bad was bound to happen.

Therapy was definitely a good idea.

"I can help you with the website for your traps in exchange for helping me study."

I kissed her impulsively. "Sounds like a plan."

She blinked at me, stunned, and then a smile bloomed on her face. "Good. One more thing."

Our plates arrived and she immediately dove into her biscuits and gravy.

"What's that?"

"Can you teach me how to ride your motorcycle?"

I wasn't expecting that. She stole a piece of bacon from my plate and I made a face.

"Yeah, I'll teach you how to ride. I think I'll enjoy that. Get you an entire leather outfit." I pictured her ass in leather pants and I almost slid out of the booth.

"It terrifies me, which is why I think I should do it. You should always do things that scare you the most. Never live your life in fear." It reminded me of something I'd said to her on that first night when Dolly had run up on my porch.

"You're exactly right," I said. "No fear, just faith."

"I love that, and I love you. And I love these." She

pointed her fork at the biscuits and then shoved nearly a whole one in her face. She really was hungry.

"I love you," I said. I'd never get sick of saying it to her.

I dropped Iris off after she demolished her huge breakfast, and she groaned when she got off the bike.

"I don't know how I'm going to make it through my shift, but a lot of coffee is going to be involved." She yawned again and I wanted to kiss her, but I had the feeling her dad was watching through the window, so I didn't, but then she grabbed the lapels of my jacket and pulled me in anyway.

I didn't hear the door open, but I did hear Kevin yelling, "It's about damn time!"

Iris and I broke apart and found Kevin standing in the doorway of the house and grinning. He gave both of us a thumbs-up.

"Oh god, I think I've died," Iris said, but I just gave Kevin a little wave and tried not to blush.

Iris hid her head against my chest and Kevin chuckled before heading back into the house.

"Well, I guess my parents know now. I bet he's texting my mom right now. I have some bad news." She looked up at me and I gazed down into the face of the woman I adored.

"What's that?" I said.

"You're going to have to come over for dinner more often."

I burst out laughing.

"That's okay. I like your parents more than I like mine."

"You wouldn't if they were your parents."

I stared at her. "That doesn't make any sense," I said.

"That doesn't matter because you love me," she said.

"Yeah, I do."

She left me to go change and take care of her dad and take a nap before she went to work. I was completely energized when I went back into the house and headed to the basement to make another lobster trap coffee table. I'd actually talked to someone at one of the local gift shops and she said that she might want to stock them, once I had enough finished to do regular orders. I had an appointment to take a few over next week.

I wanted to create. I wanted to do more. I wanted to finish the house with Iris. I wanted to sleep more. I wanted to live again.

All thanks to her.

"I miss you, Grace," I said. "I miss you, but I know you'd be happy for me. I know you'd love her. I know you still love me, and I'll always love you." It was complicated, holding a place in my heart for Grace even while I gave the rest of it to Iris. Too much love for one person, for one life, but I wasn't going to take it for granted. I was going to love. I was going to *live*.

My phone vibrated and I saw that I had a text message from Iris.

"How do you spell 'love'?" Piglet said.
"You don't spell it, you feel it," Pooh said.
Just thinking about you. I'll see you tonight, Jude.

I stared at the message and smiled. That was definitely another quote for the wall. Definitely the bedroom.

I wanted to do something for Iris, so after I worked on the second lobster trap coffee table for a little while, I went out shopping and got a bunch of things, including lobster. I hadn't paid money for it in years, and it was a strange feeling, but I wanted to make her the first meal I'd cooked for her again.

She wasn't going to get back from work until after nine, but I was going to be ready for her.

I bought candles and wine and chocolate and even made a playlist. I had never been really romantic like this, but Iris made me want to be corny and sappy and silly and traditional.

I texted her to come over after she'd seen her mom and said good-night to both of her parents, and then fretted and worried that she'd hate everything.

"Hey," she said, coming through the front door. "I'm dogless tonight, so we won't have to worry." I was waiting in the kitchen when she walked in.

"Holy shit," she said, stopping and staring.

I'd lit white tapers on the table, had laid everything out, and I'd also dressed up. She'd never seen me in anything but casual clothes, but I'd pulled out one of my suits, along with a plain white T-shirt because I couldn't go completely formal, ever.

"You look so fucking hot," she said. She still had her work clothes on, as if she hadn't wanted to take time to change or shower.

"Thank you?" I said with a laugh.

"And dinner? You are perfect. You're perfect." She came over to give me a kiss. "But you could have given me some warning. I'm completely underdressed. Can you give me ten so I can run back home and change?" The food would keep, so I said she could and she ran back over to her parents' house. When she came back I was the stunned one.

"You like?" Her dress was low-cut and made of dark blue velvet that shimmered a little in the light. She'd taken her hair down and it hung loosely on her shoulders. If I wasn't mistaken, she'd put on a little bit of mascara and a lip stain.

"I love," I said. "Love, love, love." I held my arms open for her and she hugged me.

"I love, love, love you. How was the rest of your day?" I chatted about this and that and she told me work stories and it was wonderful. I didn't think about the food or the wine (I'd poured beer into a wineglass because some things didn't change), and I felt complete peace.

"You're smiling," Iris said.

"I'm happy," I replied.

It was the truth.

Epilogue

Iris

"I can't believe you talked me into this," Jude said as we stood outside the library on a Wednesday night a few weeks later. I'd been coming every week to the queer group and had finally talked her into coming. It might have taken me flashing my breasts a little and some begging, but she was here.

"You're going to love it, I promise. Gladys and Mary are amazing, and then there's Jason and his partner, Dave. And then there's Marina and Jace. I'm going to try and be friends with her, I guess." I cringed at the thought, but in my gut, I knew it was the right thing to do. But the second she acted like a bitch? Over. Done.

Jude had changed so much in such a short period of time. She'd gotten her website up and running and had sold five of her trap coffee tables so far, with orders for more than she could make, and she was also supplying a local gift shop that was taking in more orders. I was helping her source more used traps, along with studying and working. It was a lot, but we still made time to see each other and have incredible sex. My parents had already adopted her as their second daughter and in a week, I was moving next door with Jude.

I'd started my real estate classes and there were all kinds of people, including one of the lobstermen that Jude hung out with. He said he wanted to get out of the business and his wife already had her license, so they wanted to work together. There was another guy, Cole, that I'd gone to high school with. He hadn't been a complete asshole, and he'd moved back to take care of his mom who was dealing with rheumatoid arthritis. All kinds of people came back to Salty Cove for all kinds of reasons. Jude and I were building a life here, and I can't say that it was what I planned for my life, but why was that a bad thing? I couldn't have planned Jude.

Sure, it was probably too soon to move in together for other people, but it wasn't too soon for us. We did everything in our own timing, and this timing was right.

"Come on, Jude. They're not going to bite. Unless you ask them to." I bumped her hip with mine.

"The only one I want biting me is you," she said, grinning down at me. I kissed her hard, and thought about asking her to skip the group and take me home, but this was important. Community and friends were important.

"I'll do that later," I said in her ear before nipping at her earlobe.

"Looking forward to it." She glanced back at the library and squared her shoulders. "Let's do this. Let's be social."

"Just remember that you love me," I said.

"How could I forget?"

We walked together up the steps and into the library.

"Finally," Gladys said, coming over to give me a hug. Her wife, Mary, who was the principal of the elementary school, came over and hugged me as well. They were my favorite older couple, other than my parents.

"This is Jude," I said, presenting her. Her jaw was clenched, but she shook everyone's hand.

We were going to be fine.

We all mingled and had snacks and Jude got introduced to everyone. We hung around at the end as Gladys was telling a story about meeting Mary for the first time, and Jude looked over at me with a smile on her face.

"Thank you for making me come. It's good to be around people." We'd both isolated ourselves for different reasons, but it didn't work. It never worked to go it alone.

"You're welcome," I said. "Thank you for coming."

"Thank you for loving me."

"You don't need to thank me for that. I couldn't stop

if I wanted to. And I very much don't want to ever stop loving you."

She pressed her forehead to mine. "Same."

* * * * *

Reviews are an invaluable tool when it comes to spreading the word about great reads. Please consider leaving an honest review for this, or any of Carina Press's other titles that you've read, on your favorite retail or review site.

To read more books from New York Times
bestselling author Chelsea M. Cameron,
please visit her website:

chelseamcameron.com

Acknowledgments

It's been a long time since I've written these for a tradition-ally published book. I feel like I'm a little rusty, but let's start with the basics: Thank you to my editor, Carrie Lofty, and the entire Carina team, especially everyone from Adores, for seeing something in this story and giving me a chance. Special thanks to the cover design team, the copy editors, and the publicity team as well. You are the unsung heroes!

Thanks also to my fabulous author friends (you know who you are), who keep me going and keep me laugh-ing and make me feel like I'm not alone in this ridiculous career. Thanks to everyone who supports me on social media. You all help me more than you know. Thank you to my Patrons and my super readers who have been with me through thick and thin. You help me keep going, even when the going gets tough. A debt of gratitude to all the readers who said "YES!" when I asked if this book was something they'd want to read.

I also can't leave out my family, especially my mom. I can't neglect my IRL friends, and my yoga family for always being unfailingly supportive of my books and my writing. I wrote this book during a time in my life when I wasn't sure I could believe in romance again, but I took the journey with Iris and Jude and it helped me believe again. If this book has done even a fraction of that for you, then I've done my job.

*Vince Amato is back in New Hope to flip
The Hideaway Inn to the highest bidder and return ASAP to
his luxury lifestyle in New York City. But Vince gets stuck in
the middle of nowhere, and Tack O'Leary,
the gorgeous, easygoing farm boy who broke his heart years ago
is the only person who can help.*

Keep reading for an excerpt of
The Hideaway Inn
*by Philip William Stover,
out now from Carina Adores!*

Chapter One

"This isn't New Hope," I tell the bus driver.

"No, it's Pittstown. Last stop."

Back in Manhattan a company chauffeur takes me wherever I need to go but I do pass by plenty of bus stops—little huts with glass walls and cologne ads. Those are bus stops. This isn't a bus stop. It's a cow pasture.

The driver opens the door and the smell of manure is so strong I have to hold the pocket square from my suit jacket over my mouth to stop from gagging.

"Memorial Day weekend schedule. Bus doesn't go all the way to New Hope. Last stop is here, Pittstown."

I look out the window. Cows to the right, empty fields to the left and nothing ahead of me or behind. Dark clouds gather in the sky, threatening an early summer rainstorm.

My first thought is to just throw some money at the guy and bark at him to do what I want but those days are on pause, at least for now.

"Come on, man. My phone's dead. Call an Uber for me?" At this point I'm almost whining, something I never do, but I've been doing a lot of things I never do lately.

"We don't have Uber. You aren't from around here?" He examines me over his sunglasses.

The truth is, I grew up about twenty miles away in a town where the Jersey suburbs rubbed up against the Garden State farmlands. Everything east of that was big box stores and gas stations, everything west was rolling farmland. I pretty much spent my childhood reading overly sentimental verse or searching online for an acne cure.

"No, I'm not."

"There's a general store about six miles ahead. They might be able to call you a cab."

I grab my shoulder bag, thank the guy—for what, I don't know—and step off the bus straight into a puddle of mud. The bus releases its brakes with a hiss of air and then disappears over the hill. I'm alone on the side of the road wearing a three-thousand-dollar bespoke suit and nine-hundred-dollar shoes, covered in mud.

After walking over a mile without passing any living thing except a number of cows who I swear give me dirty looks, a pickup truck zooms past me on a blind curve only to pump the brakes when a bale of hay falls off the back. This could be my ticket out of my misery. With any luck this hick will be a serial killer and he'll see the word *next* written all over me. If that doesn't work out I guess I could ask him to take me to the general store.

I start jogging toward the truck but as the guy steps out, I stop immediately. He's far away but I can see that he is no stranger to hard labor. He's wearing jeans so tight even from this distance I can see that each cheek of his bubble butt is a perfectly proportioned independent entity. Even though it's a chilly sunless day he has his flannel shirt tied around his waist so his tank top reveals sun kissed arms that are thick from what I imagine to be hours of work in the fields. A trucker hat and sunglasses cover his face but that body is enough to turn this whole day around.

I pick up my pace and walk toward the truck. The guy throws a rope around the hay bales in the cargo bed and moves to the other side to secure them.

"Excuse me," I say, and my deep voice booms across the field. I know the effect it usually has on people. At the firm, it made people follow my orders and in bed it does the same thing. It may be a polished performance, but it has great effect.

"Hold up," he says from the other side of the truck. His voice is deep but not as heavy as mine and with less gravel. I hear him fiddling with the rope and can see the hair on his toned arms glisten in the late morning sunlight. I'm already picturing a handsome boyish face with a wide confident smile. I hear the ground crunch under his feet as he walks toward my side of the truck.

He takes one look at me and stops. "No way!" he says.

He pulls off his hay-dusted sunglasses. "Skinny Vinny. What the hell are you doing here?"

My body freezes. I can't believe who I'm seeing. It's been over fifteen years, but the sight of him has me feeling like the skinny geeky kid with the impossible crush.

I quickly gather myself and immediately correct him. "It's Vince now. Vince," I say, my lips vibrating against my teeth firmly as I make sure my voice is deeper and stronger than it is in even my most alpha moments. The shock of seeing him has my heart racing, but I'm an expert at covering weak emotions—on the rare occasions that I have them.

I can't believe this guy recognized me?

I spent the decade and a half that I've been away from this area working on the transformation. I put on at least twenty pounds of pure muscle, my beard has grown to a controlled scruff, and daily-wear contacts mean my dark-brown eyes don't hide behind lenses thicker than hickory bacon. Not to mention that every breath I take is a controlled study in hyper-masculinity, from my voice to how I hold my body to my lack of overly expressive emotion. This is Vince. I'm Vince. I'll never be Skinny Vinny again.

"Do I know you?" I ask. He looks exactly the same, maybe even hotter, but I don't want him to think he was ever significant to me. Even though he has had more than an occasional role in my jerk-off fantasies since I was a teenager.

"Come on, it hasn't been that long. It's me, Tack. Tack O'Leary. And, ah, yeah, I'm still Tack," he says. Of course, Tack hasn't had to change a thing about himself since high school including being named after the equipment used on his beloved horses. He was voted Most Popular, Most Athletic and Nicest Eyes. Usually they only let you win in one category but Tack's year was such a landslide they bent the rules. I would have been voted Most Likely to Not be Voted Anything if that was a category since the only people who really knew me were the boys who teased me relentlessly for being a "girly-boy." No one would call me that now.

"Oh, right. I remember now. Your family had a farm," I say, keeping up my charade by pretending to piece the details together in my head and trying not to look at the outline of his dick in his pants. I respect having a great dick or a great ass but having both is really just obnoxious.

"Still do. I've got a load of fresh eggs and some produce under all that hay. I'm taking it to the farmers market in New Hope. But what the hell are you doing in the middle of Route 513 in Pittstown?"

Tack looks me up and down and I can't tell if he is examining my hard-earned muscular body or the fact that I'm dressed for a board meeting, not the side of a country road. I got on the bus right after signing the summer rental agreement with the tenants for my penthouse. I wanted to give them the impression that I was still a powerful master of the universe so they wouldn't balk at the incredibly high monthly charge. They didn't need to know that without the rent money, I would default on the apartment's second mortgage that I'm using to renovate the place in New Hope. A buddy gave me an inside tip about an investment opportunity and I wasn't in a position to be picky about the location.

"I'm actually headed to New Hope," I say, but as soon as the words come out of my mouth I realize I should have given a different answer. Now it sounds like I want a ride, which I do but *not* with him. I'd rather crawl to New Hope on my hands and knees. But first, I would change my pants because they cost more than his beat-up truck.

"Looks like you need a ride," he says. His mouth closes and one side of his smile tightens to show off a sexy grin.

No. There is no way I am getting in that truck with Tack. He is the very last person I wanted to see here. Does Tack know he broke my heart? Does he even remember what he did to me? Inside I'm an almost uncontrollable storm of lust, regret, fear and desire but I take every last feeling and stuff it deep beneath my exterior. Vinny might babble a string of needy requests but Vince knows how to focus and turn the tables.

"Question is," I say, making sure my face remains without expression, "why is Tack O'Leary going to New Hope? Didn't your buddies always say that place was full of queers?"

"Still is," he says without missing a beat. "Some things are still the same but a lot of things aren't." Tack always spoke in riddles. It's just as annoying as ever. "New Hope has the most popular farmers market in all of Bucks County. I'm there helping sell my dad's produce when I have time."

"How is your dad?" I ask just to be polite. Mr. O'Leary

was an asshole of major proportions. I'm sure as he has gotten older, he's gotten even more zealous.

"He's the same," Tack says without emotion. "I gotta get going. You in or not?" The tone of Tack's voice either shows he's in a hurry or that asking about his dad hit a raw spot.

"I'll just walk to the general store up ahead and call a cab. Good luck with your hay, Tack," I say, hoping my tone conveys fuck off.

Tack steps toward me and I can smell the potent mix of sweat and hay on his skin. Reminds me of visits to his farm in high school and waiting for him to finish his chores so we could... I get an immediate semi that I reposition as best I can down the side of my leg so it isn't too obvious.

He walks closer to the truck, stretches his arm in front of me and then opens the passenger side door.

"Get in," he says.

"Like I said, I'm just going to..."

"The general store is closed for renovations and there hasn't been a pay phone there for like ten years." He looks me up and down again. I'm sure he can see my pulsing erection and this time I don't care. Let him see how big it is. Let him see the man I've become. I know he doesn't want to be with me. He made that very clear many years ago. But I don't care. Let him see what he's been missing.

"Get in," he says again, but this time his voice doesn't have any edge.

Against my better judgment, I jump in his vintage pickup

truck without saying a word. Once I'm in, he slams the door, and lets that sexy smile linger.

"Next stop, New Hope."

Chapter Two

As soon as we make it over the hill, the expansive countryside opens before me like an antique quilt unfolding at a county fair. Recently mowed fields make perfectly parallel lines that bend with the shape of the land; yellow grassy patches are contained by split rail fences so farm animals can freely graze; newly green trees create small clusters of forest. I never appreciated the beauty of the countryside as a kid.

It would almost feel calm and peaceful if riding in Tack's pickup didn't feel like being put in a cardboard box and kicked across a field. We bump and bounce over every pothole. I'm a few inches taller than Tack and I think he's enjoying making sure my head hits the roof of the cab whenever he can make it happen.

"Do you have to hit every pothole in the road?" I ask.

"It was a rough winter. Roads are still torn up," he says. He glances over at me for a second but I spot a huge ditch ahead.

"Watch out!" I shout with more inflection than I would like. Tack suddenly swerves to avoid the crater and the momentum makes me slide across the bench and right into Tack. For just a second my face brushes against his shoulder. The feel of his body is exhilarating and awkward all at once. I immediately push myself back to the passenger side and fasten my seat belt so it won't happen again. He doesn't say anything but I think I see a smile approach his lips. Tack stares straight ahead; his focus is on the road.

We ride in silence which I am sure surprises him. In high school, I'd blather on about some random poem I loved or a character in a book I was reading. As an adult I learned the power of silence. It can make people uncomfortable and you can use that to your advantage.

I keep my eyes forward without saying a word. I force Tack to make the first move to start a conversation. Let him understand who is in control now. We travel through the countryside and down to the road that hugs the river. It's early summer so the trees are bare enough that I can see the small currents and rapids that punctuate the glassy surface of the Delaware.

"So, you going to New Hope for the weekend or something?" Tack says, caving to the silence.

"Not exactly."

"Well, the radio is broke and we got a slow ten miles until we get there. Maybe you can tell me what the hell you're doing here after, what, more than fifteen years?" I look over at him and I can't tell if he is angry or teasing. Since he's focused on the road I can take a longer look than before. His dirty blond hair has darkened just a bit and his face has filled out so that his chin is even stronger and his jawline even sharper. He looks like he should be on a calendar featuring super-hot farmers.

"So, are you gonna tell me?" he asks.

I snap out of my fantasy and refocus. "Oh, yeah, sure. I mean, I can. No problem." I'm all stumbles and hesitation. That's not Vince, that's Vinny. This guy's got me losing my edge in less than five minutes in his presence. I order myself to pull it together.

"There was an investment opportunity right on the river. Great little inn that fell on hard times. Owners couldn't keep it going so when the deal came across my desk, I realized it had a great ROI." I look at him and jump on this opportunity to show off who I am now. "*That's return on investment*," I say slowly but he doesn't take the bait.

"Got it," he says, staring straight ahead.

Most of what I've told him is true. Not that I'm worried about lying to Tack—he never did place a whole lot of emphasis on telling the truth. I don't tell him that I lost my fortune in a deal that went south after the firm found out I had been fucking one of the biggest investors. I don't tell him my buddy pointed me in the direction of this deal because he knew a hospitality chain was developing a plan to buy a bunch of charming inns and make a conglomerate. I don't tell him how desperate I am to make sure this one shows a profit so that by the end of the summer Fun-

Tyme Inc. will want to add this inn their portfolio and I'll be able to cash out and get back to New York.

I sold off all my toys that had price tags over four figures, rented out my penthouse and decided to come out here just for the summer so I could flip this place, make a huge profit, get back on my feet and go back to New York City.

"And you?" I ask, changing the subject. What have you been up to?" I don't want to ask it but the next question just falls out of my mouth and I can't stop it. "What happened with you and Evie?" I squeeze my hands into a fist after the question comes out and dig my nails into my hand. Why would I give him even the slightest indication that I care about him and Evie?

"I was wondering when you would ask that," he says. *Oh, screw you, Tack.* I stare straight ahead.

"Just making conversation," I say, throwing the line away, my voice perfectly steady and without a hint of inflection.

"Sure," he says. "Well, about a year or so after high school we got hitched."

"I see." I make sure I show zero emotion on the outside. My insides, though, crash with the pain of knowing, without a doubt, that he never wanted and never could want me. The rejection still smacks me in the heart and makes me feel like a bale of hay he doesn't even know has fallen off his truck.

I look out the window and see the river hug a small, newly green island in the middle of the flow. It's been fifteen years and I'll be here for just the season. What do I care about him and Evie? It doesn't matter how much I wanted Tack, how often I thought about him or how perfect I thought our lives could be together. It's not what he wanted. He made that clear; I guess I just never let myself picture them actually getting married. "I know that's what you always wanted."

"It was. By the way, which place in New Hope? The one between the playhouse and the water?" I'm totally fine with him being the one to change that rancid subject.

"Yeah, The Hideaway Inn. There's a big Memorial Day weekend luncheon this afternoon in the restaurant."

"The Hideaway? People have been calling that the *Hide-a-went*. They haven't seen a guest at that place for years. Restaurant is still open though."

"Thank you, Tack. I am aware."

"Have you seen it recently, though?"

"No. Closed-bid auction. All online. Sight unseen."

"Oh..." His eyes widen like I just said I purchased an ancient ruin.

"What's that supposed to mean?"

"Ah, nothing." There is a slight but noticeable mocking laugh in his voice.

"Look, stop being an asshole," I say.

"Asshole? I'm the one who picked you up off the side of the road."

"Yeah, well, you are also the one who..." I'm about to bring up the past when I see a sign on the road that reads "New Hope, this way." Tack takes the turn. "Never mind," I say and we go back to a chilly silence.

We cross over from New Jersey to Pennsylvania on the New Hope–Lambertville Bridge. New Hope looks like something out of a Norman Rockwell painting—small, boldly painted colonial-style buildings line a river walk with trees, fountains and a gazebo. The historic Bucks County Playhouse that was once a gristmill proudly anchors the landscape.

As we turn on to Main Street I realize that the town is more like a Norman Rockwell painting if old Norm had been a power-bottom with a social activist consciousness. Rainbow flags hang from almost every storefront, same-sex couples walk hand in hand and "Love is love" signs cover the town like it's a mandatory municipal ordinance.

"Never any place to park in this town. Okay to use the parking at the Hide-a-went?" Tack asks.

"Sure," I say. "But if you call it that again I'll make sure you're towed into the Delaware." I'm kidding, of course, I wouldn't have his truck towed into the river. I'd just push it in myself.

Tack pulls in front of The Hideaway Inn and I see my investment for the first time. A three-story stately stone home that, according to my research, was built in the mid-eighteenth century by a wealthy farmer who wanted to have a place on the river away from his crops. I imagine he also had some side-action in town. There are more windows than a typical structure from the time period, and the previous owner blew out the back of the place so that the dining area and guest rooms have huge, expansive windows and a sundeck with amazing views of the river.

Once Tack pulls into the tiny lot I grab my bag and get out of the truck. "I won't be parked long, just need to drop these vegetables and eggs off at the Ferry Market on the next block," he says. "See you around."

"Sure," I say and watch him walk away carrying a crate of produce that make his triceps flex so hard they look like sleek torpedoes ready to be fired. No. I will not spend the summer lusting after Tack. Again. I'll make sure I don't see Tack again while I'm in New Hope. I'll avoid him with the same enthusiasm I avoid Porta Potties at outdoor music festivals. If I do run into him on the street I'll simply run into oncoming traffic or set myself on fire. My latest, and currently sole, investment is right in front of me. Time to start understanding what I've gotten myself into.

On closer inspection of the inn, I notice a few details that I need to take care of: painting the peeling trim with a brighter color, fixing the blue shutters that cling to the edges of the windows like their lives depend on it, and getting rid of those garish pride flags that make the place look cluttered. I look up to the third floor where the owner's suite is located and make a mental note to replant the window boxes with red geraniums before the weeds reach past the windows.

I look at my watch and realize I only have about forty minutes until the LGBTQ Historical Society arrives for their annual Memorial Day Weekend luncheon. While the guest rooms have been closed for some time, the cafe has been running continuously thanks to the dedication of the restaurant manager, Anita Patel, who I have been phoning and emailing with since the sale. She impressed me with her no-nonsense attitude even if she thinks I work for her rather than the other way around. She thought this luncheon would be a good way to introduce the new ownership and get to know the most powerful LGBTQ community members. I just wanted to know how much we were charging and the bottom-line profit for the event. Anita avoided a real answer but mentioned a "community discount" for the group, which I honored, but that won't be happening again. It's a business, not a charity.

I open the front door to the cafe. Ruffled burgundy curtains that look like they were put up the night disco was invented sag over the windows and shabby white napkins sit sadly on threadbare tablecloths. Some of the walls are painted a cheery yellow. Others have wallpaper from what must have been an ancient asylum for the criminally ugly and still others are painted bright blue. It's the opposite of my favorite places in New York, all of which have dark colors and stark exposed steel beams. Still, there is a part deep inside me that finds this place cozy and warm. There is even a crackling fire in the massive brick fireplace that covers the entire back wall and it helps take off the late-May chill. The place definitely needs a good deal of work but that's what I'm here to do.

BOOM!

A small hydrogen bomb has exploded. I walk toward the sound and swing open the door to the kitchen. A woman in chef's gear and an older, slightly frail man wearing a waiter's uniform are standing a few inches from each other, arguing. The floor is covered with cookware, trays and what look like raw Cornish game hens.

"What the fuck?" I shout as I barge through the doors.

"I cannot work with this imbecile anymore. He ruined the entire meal," the woman in the chef's uniform barks at me. "We have nothing to serve to half the guests!" Carla. The chef. Anita had described her as small but tightly wound.

"You weren't paying attention *as usual* and knocked over the tray. I wasn't even on that side of the kitchen, dearie," the man says, his tone as pointed as a needle. He must be Clayton the waiter.

"Where's Anita?" I demand, looking at the clock above the back door and realizing we don't have much time until the luncheon.

"Who are you?" Carla asks in full attack mode.

"I'm Vince," I shoot back at her. "The new owner."

"Great. The first thing you can do is fire him. Now!" Chef Carla points at Clayton, who gives me a look like someone ran over his cat.

"I have been at this cafe over twenty years. How dare you," he says.

"How dare I? I'm the chef," Carla retorts.

"Let's all stay calm," I say, despite the fact that it feels like things are already out of control. "We have some important guests arriving very soon. Let's work this out *after* we have a successful lunch."

More general screaming between the two erupts.

Oh, hell no. "Stop it!" I finally shout louder than both of them. They shut up immediately.

Chef Carla points her finger at me. "I do not want that man in my kitchen one second longer. Fire him. Now!"

I do not do well with people telling me what to do. At.
All. "We will work this out *after* lunch, *I said*."

There is a moment of silence and then Carla unties her
apron and throws it on the ground.

Oh no.

"I have worked in kitchens up and down the river and I re-
fuse to have my authority undermined. I am the chef. What I
say is law. Maybe you don't understand how a kitchen works."

She couldn't be more right but I'm not about to let her
know that.

"I quit!" she shouts and walks out the door.

Normally if someone under me threw a tantrum like that
I would hold the door open for them as they walked out,
but with guests about to arrive, I need her. The last meal
I cooked involved a microwave and soggy leftover pizza.

I walk out the back door of the kitchen and run after
her. "Carla, wait!" I say but she quickly barrels down Main
Street. "Carla!" I yell but she is too far away or pretending
not to hear me. Either way, I'm screwed. I yell out, "Carla!
Carla!" like I am looking for a lost dog. A few people stare
at me and I don't think it can get much worse until something rolls over my left foot.

Don't miss The Hideaway Inn,
Book One of Seasons of New Hope
by Philip William Stover!
www.CarinaPress.com

Also available from New York Times bestselling author
Chelsea M. Cameron:

Anyone But You

Things are going great for Sutton Kay, or at least they were. Her yoga studio is doing well, she's living with her best friend, and she just got two kittens named Mocha and Cappuccino. Sure, she doesn't have a girlfriend, but her life is full and busy.

Then her building is sold and the new landlord turns out to be the woman putting in a gym downstairs who doesn't seem to understand the concepts "courtesy" and "don't be rude to your tenants." Sutton can't get a read on Tuesday Grímsdóttir, but she can appreciate her muscles. Seriously, Tuesday is ripped. Not that that has anything to do with anything since she's too surly to have a conversation with, and won't stop pissing Sutton off.

Sutton's life gets interesting after she dares Tuesday to make it through one yoga class, and then Tuesday gives Sutton a similar dare. Soon enough they're spending time working out together and when the sweat starts flowing, the sparks start flying. How is it possible to be so attracted to a person you can barely stand?

But when someone from Tuesday's past shows up and Sutton sees a whole new side of Tuesday, will she change her mind about her grumpy landlord? Can she?

To read more from Chelsea M. Cameron,
visit her website:
chelseamcameron.com

Discover another heartwarming small-town romance from Carina Adores.

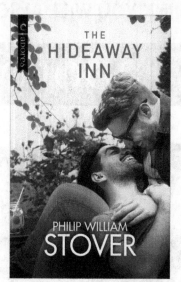

No one in the charming river town of New Hope, Pennsylvania, needs to know that Vince Amato plans on flipping the Hideaway Inn to the highest bidder and returning to his luxury lifestyle in New York City. He needs to make his last remaining investment turn a profit…even if that means temporarily relocating to the quirky small town where he endured growing up.

But he didn't count on Tack O'Leary, the gorgeous, easygoing farm boy who broke his heart years ago, signing on to be the chef at the inn for the summer.

As Vince and Tack open their hearts to each other again, Vince learns that being true to himself doesn't mean shutting down a second chance with Tack—it means starting over and letting love in.

The Hideaway Inn by **Philip William Stover**

Available now!

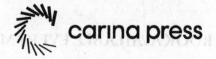

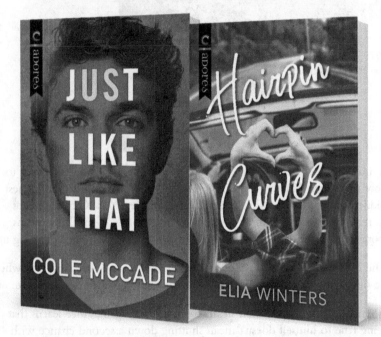